D0355836

Kirsten Ekman is Sweden's most prominent female fiction writer, with many novels to her name, and winner of many literary awards, including the Great Prize for Fiction (1977), the August Prize (1993), the Nordic Council Prize (1994) and the Pilot Prize (1995).

THE DOG

KERSTIN EKMAN

Translated from the Swedish by
Linda Schenck and Rochelle Wright

SPHERE

First published as *Hunden* in Sweden in 1986 by Bonniers
First published in Great Britain in 2009 by Sphere
This paperback edition published in 2010 by Sphere
Reprinted by Sphere in 2011

Published by arrangement with Bonnier Group Agency, Stockholm, Sweden.

The moral right of the author has been asserted.

*All characters and events in this publication, other than those
clearly in the public domain, are fictitious and any resemblance
to real persons, living or dead, is purely coincidental.*

A CIP catalogue record for this book
is available from the British Library.

ISBN 978-0-7515-4050-5

Typeset in Bembo by M Rules
Printed and bound in Great Britain by
Clays Ltd, St Ives plc

Papers used by Sphere are natural, renewable and
recyclable products sourced from well-managed forests and certified
in accordance with the rules of the Forest Stewardship Council.

Mixed Sources
Product group from well-managed
forests and other controlled sources
www.fsc.org Cert no. SGS-COC-004081
© 1996 Forest Stewardship Council
FSC

Sphere
An imprint of
Little, Brown Book Group
100 Victoria Embankment
London EC4Y 0DY

An Hachette UK Company
www.hachette.co.uk

www.littlebrown.co.uk

When does something begin?

It doesn't begin. There's always something else before it. It begins the way a stream starts as a rivulet and a rivulet starts as a trickle of water in the marsh. It's the rain that makes the marsh water rise.

In winter the spruces have full skirts. The snow is so deep that it catches in the bottom ring of branches. When storms pack it down, hollows and dens form under the trees. A fox can find a hideout there, out of the wind and foul weather. Grouse hens take cover under the skirts of the spruces too, but never under the same root as the fox. He huddles there waiting for night to fall. He waits for the moonlight and for a crust to form on the snow.

★

Where does a tale begin?

Under the root of a spruce, perhaps.

Yes, under the root of a spruce tree. A little grey fellow was lying there, all curled up, his muzzle tucked under his tail. A dog. But he didn't know that. He was so small he was able to squeeze in under a root. The root encircled him like a rough brown arm but it didn't keep him warm.

The only warmth he got was from his own body. Inside him was emptiness. He couldn't think: warmth, belly, teats, milk. He didn't remember his mother's belly with its thin, white coat, or her yellow eyes gleaming when they all suckled.

He couldn't remember. There was nothing but a great big hole inside, a gnawing, a hunger for warmth and for the mild, pungent sweetness that filled his mouth, and for his mother when she had come in from outside with strange scents in her fur, nipping at the scruff of his neck and licking the corner of his mouth.

How had he ended up under that spruce?

He didn't remember and he couldn't have told the tale.

The man headed out on to the frozen lake on his snowmobile. He was going fishing. The mother dog had seen him take his green jacket from the hook and figured he was going hunting. It was the wrong time of year, though; the scent of the March air told her that. She sat on the front steps, quiet and attentive. When the snowmobile swung out behind the woodshed she thought she saw the butt of a rifle, but her sight wasn't very good. It was the ice drill he had strapped onto his backpack. He hadn't called her to him. He hadn't signalled his plans. But the green jacket, the rifle butt. She sat rigid, ears cocked, until the snowmobile vanished in among the pine trees by the marsh. Then she bounded off after him anyway. The hunt!

And behind her, the pup.

It was a wide path, rough from snowmobile tracks. He could smell petrol and oil and his mother. He ran, barrelling along on his short legs. Soon she was out of sight, though he could still hear the engine. Then there was silence and he was alone on the long, white ribbon leading out on to the lake.

The man drove across the lake to the boat landing by the summer pasture, and looped up to the cabin to check that things were all right. Then back down to the lake. He didn't see the dog following him until he stopped. By the time she caught up she was worn out. Her belly sagged under her. You silly girl, he said. I'll bet you thought I was going hunting!

He started drilling through the new ice over the fishing holes, and set the lines in place. The air was piercing cold, the mist so thick he couldn't see the mountain tops. The dog sat beside him, her yellow eyes squinting. Her sensitive nose caught the scent of her pup, and every now and then she took a turn round the fishing holes, expecting him to come. The fish weren't biting and the cold, black water froze in layers of ice on the fishing lines.

A flurry of snow, a grey swirl, passed over the lake. She snorted. Her master said, We'd best be heading home. He took it slowly enough for her to keep up. But he drove back in a wide arc, not the same way he had come.

When the man returned his wife was on the front steps, her hands up the sleeves of her sweater. By then there was driving snow and a hard westerly wind off the mountains in Norway. She told him one of the pups was missing. The dark grey one.

They searched all day in the powdery, whirling snow. They tried to get the mother dog to follow his scent but she couldn't. The snow didn't let up. By evening it had become a storm. His wife wept, saying they'd never find the pup. He'll have frozen to death by now, she said.

A storm from the west is like a broom, a grey blast sweeping across lake and forest. Afterwards there's no trace of ski or snowmobile tracks, of animal or bird, no wads of snuff around the fishing holes, no bait, no blood. Everything is fresh, white and smooth.

Now, the morning after the storm, no one could see the tracks from the man on the snowmobile. The weather had cleared. The sun hadn't yet risen and the sky shifted towards green as the day grew light. The sliver of moon above the hill faded. It looked tenuous and tattered.

A black grouse flew up. The snow whirled around his wings when he burst out from his hollow under the spruce. He settled high up in a birch and soon there came another and yet another. They clung there like dark fruit in the crown of the birch, so heavy the branches sagged under them. They began eating leaf buds.

The pup had slept under his spruce. He was stiff and thirsty when he crawled out and lifted his nose above the newly fallen snow. The light, what little there was, blinded him. He saw the grouse in the birch tree but didn't know what they were or whether they were dangerous. They were alive. In the whiteness their black heads were the only thing moving. He crept backwards into the hole and ate snow. It triggered his hunger, and his stomach began to ache. He whined but no one came. He whimpered, listening. No paws crossing the linoleum, no boot steps, no voice.

He slept a little but the bellyache was still there and made him whine. The next time he awakened he thought he picked up a smell that wasn't like snow or cold or air, and he started digging. He kicked up pine needles and soil and then finally found what he'd smelled. He kept at it for a long time and when the sun came up and gleamed in the icy windows of the pasture cabin he had eaten two fox turds and a few lingonberries.

When he next woke up the grouse were gone. Sunlight glared off the snow and he squinted with pain. He shut his eyes and ate some snow; it melted quickly in his mouth.

Water from the thawing snow ran into the hole. Now he was really freezing because his fur, still a puppy coat, was soaked through.

A magpie flashed across his field of vision and settled not far away; he could hear her chatter and peck.

He recognised the sound. Magpie chatter was followed by the mother dog's growling when the bright bird grew bold and came too close to their food. Insistent, penetrating sounds were also what he longed for: his mother and the food bowl. He wanted to get back. But when he started off through the damp snow he sank, floundering. Soon everything was just wet and grey and he was exhausted. He lay deep in the snow for a long time, without hearing the magpie. Then the memory faded. When he really started to freeze, with his bare belly against the wet snow, he managed, even though his legs hurt, to turn around and make his way back to the hole under the spruce.

He slept, and even when the sun was at its highest in the sky it never penetrated the root of the spruce where he was lying. This was on a northern slope, on a wooded rise behind the summer pasture. Faint with hunger, he lay with his muzzle tucked under his own backside to draw warmth from his body, from his own wet, matted coat and the cavity in which his heart fluttered like the wing of a bird in the cold and damp. It beat eagerly and wildly, throbbing, hungry for life, for warmth and kind voices, for milk, sunshine, tongues, fur, paws, belly and legs.

He wasn't alone in the pasture. A squirrel scurried, hooked claws clattering on the bark of the spruce tree. The black grouse settled in the treetop again when the snow turned blue. They sat in the dusk, filling their gullets with birch buds to ward off hunger and the night and the cold that crept up from the shadows. He had heard the cheeping and twittering of a great tit all afternoon in the sunlight, and the drip of the melting snow. Now that it was colder, the bird was silent and had crept in under the eaves of the cabin. A little flock of them spent the night there, keeping each other warm.

It was a cold night. They slept under the eaves with pattering hearts, their blood coursing and throbbing. In crevices and nests, in dens and under roots they slept. The pup sank more deeply into the lethargy of cold.

★

The magpie's sharp, piercing laughter. Time after time her impudent chatter from the top of a birch. The woods near the pasture are full of other magpies and they need to know she's here, that she's claimed this treetop and everything visible from it. The others hear her but do not reply. And all the way down under the branches of the spruce tree, heavy with the weight of the frozen, wet snow, the pup hears the magpie. Eventually he comes completely awake, surfacing from a sleep that has long been dangerously deep, thanks to the cheeky, insistent jabbering.

He moves around because he's thirsty and manages to eat a bit of snow. But it isn't the same. It's hard. The magpie goes on chattering; from his hole the pup can see the flash of her white breast and the way her blue and black tail feathers shimmer with every outburst. She woke him up. The snow he ate has triggered the hunger inside him. Now he crawls out. The magpie's finished and she flies off, disappearing into the woods in a gleaming black arc.

This is a different kind of morning. Very cold, very few scents in the air. The birch branches have long, stiff icicles from snow that melted the previous day. A light breeze from the lake sets them in motion and they ring like chimes. The sharp crust of the snow cuts the pads of his paws when he pulls himself up into his old tracks. Finally he's standing on top of the snow, a frozen floor. He walks clumsily on big puppy paws. Yesterday the snow was wet and mushy. It caved in, dropping him into grey hollows where he couldn't keep his balance. Today it holds him. He barrels forward, steadier now. Sometimes he stops to lick the crust of the snow.

That morning his hunger drove him a long way, despite his exhaustion. Big drifts had blown up against the cabin. He couldn't get close to it. Slowly he continued up the hill, resting now and then on the crust, panting. He kept looking up towards the barn. When he reached it he sat down in front of the door. He looked at it. But nobody came. He yelped and whimpered but no voice answered. He curled up against the door. He didn't fall asleep but lay looking out across the marsh, sniffing. He caught a scent. Soon he also saw something white bounding through the newly planted pines. It was a hare. The pup rose stiffly and made his way down the slope. He thought that where there was movement he might find the high voice or the deep one. Or his mother. There might be food.

The scent was still there, rich and pungent among the

small pines, but the hare was long gone. At least it had left something behind. He gobbled up several pellets of warm hare droppings. He started off again in search of more. That was when he heard a voice. It was forceful and stern and kept repeating one single sound. By now he had reached the marsh, and where he was standing the birches and the little waterlogged pines were so sparse there was nowhere to hide. He crouched, belly to the snow crust, hearing the voice again. It was scolding him. When he peered up he saw outspread black wings, wings he already had inside him, an image that was deep down and signalled danger. He dragged himself towards a small pine tree but it had so few branches he could still see the silhouette of the crow. All of a sudden there were more voices and more black, circling bodies. They left him alone, though. They were after something else they couldn't find in the expanse of white, covered with a thin layer of ice, still so hard from the morning chill that it held his weight.

He padded across the snow, on his guard against the ones up there, ready to lie flat if they dive-bombed. But what made him keep going and overpowered his fear was something his sense of smell had picked up and that kept growing stronger. The scent was coming from the snow. It made him start digging with his paws and poking with his nose. The crust was sharp but he broke through it quickly and the smell, the wonderful smell, the smell of food, wafted up. The snow had receded, packed down by the thaw. It was heavy and grey but he didn't sink into it the way he had the day before. Head and forepaws deep in a hole, he dug out the snow the storm had brought. Suddenly he got his first taste of whatever had smelled so good, though it was just a little scrap. He went on digging all the way down. Finally he sank his teeth into a frozen flank with a bristly hide. He had got through. It was food.

The crows were carrying on. They saw he'd got hold of the thing they were after, concealed from them by the snowstorm. They circled closer, settling in the tops of the pines, scolding loudly. But he wasn't prey for them. When they came too close he growled, his body all muscle and determination now, arched over the big frozen mound of food in the snow. They couldn't know the white teeth he bared were just puppy teeth. Eighty-four dawns were behind him when the sun rose, and he wouldn't have made it through a single day more if he hadn't found the moose carcass in the marsh. No one can live long on hare droppings.

★

The nights were very cold. He sought shelter as close to the food supply as he could, but found none in the marsh. He had to head up the south slope where enormous spruces spread out their protective skirts. From there he could see the place where the snow was spotted with fur. At dawn, as soon as he heard the crows, he left the shelter.

In the mornings the young birches and pines were covered with white hoar frost and the crust held all the way to the food spot, where the crows were circling, flapping and screeching. A few days earlier he had cowered in fear of them. Now his belly was round and he stayed warm all night and angry all day. When he curled around himself with his muzzle tucked up under him he kept that vital spark of life burning inside. In the mornings he was hungry but not worn out. When the screeching awakened him he was cold and sluggish with sleep, but when he saw the crows sitting in the snow tearing at his food his anger woke up as well.

Within a few mornings he had realised they'd fly off when he approached, and he took the time to pee before heading toward them. Urinating on the crust of snow, crouching like a female, he glared at the big-beaked thieves.

As the sun rose higher in the sky the frost on the trees melted and dripped. By midday the water was streaming and the sun beat down. It warmed his back. Bulging with food, he needed somewhere to rest. He lay against a spruce trunk in the sun and, what with the warmth and the dizzying sense of satisfaction, he couldn't keep his eyes open, even when he heard rustling and chirping nearby. He slept in the comforting sunlight, squinting with one eye when he heard pine cones fall or branches snap. There weren't many sounds in the forest in the middle of the day. The soft chirping of the titmouse, the willow-tit's constant activity in the spruces above him. Murmuring water. Dripping branches. It made him drowsy.

In the engulfing, deep blue twilight the cold crept up stealthily. He needed to eat again. His gums were bleeding from the new teeth coming through. A fresh crust formed on the snow and at night, when the stars shone bright over the jagged spruces, the temperature dropped. He went back to his shelter and carefully chose a spot for sleep, tramping in a circle and finally curling up with a deep sigh.

Sometimes at night he heard howling. He raised his head and shivers of anticipation ran through his body. He was riveted, but as the tension receded a dull sense of discomfort was left in its wake. Only sleep could make that go away.

The howling was hoarse and piercing, carried by the wind from off the lake. It wasn't the right howl: his mother's. There was something dangerous about it that came through despite his weariness. Even in his sleep, all his muscles were quivering slightly. Finally the howling ceased. All the tension left his body and his sleep was deep and oblivious.

Day followed day and between them cold fragments of nights penetrated his sleep with the hooting of an owl or the snapping of a frozen branch. But he didn't connect the days in a series. His life and his memory were images upon images, fading in and out, scraps of days with bright skies, sharp scents to follow, disconnected cries wafting one by one through the woods until they attached to an image deep inside him. There was baying darkness that turned into grey dawn and blustering, biting snow that forced him back into the hole; there were days and nights of hunger when he shivered from the cold and damp, days of gluttony with the hot sun on his back. The others down by the marsh moved in and out of these images: a white, long-eared shape bobbing in circles among the trees; the enormous grey creatures with long legs making their way across the marsh; the screeching black forms; the little peepers and busy chatterers in the spruces; the black, heavy ones perched in the tops of the birches; other grey animals that left such straight tracks among the tree roots. He never got really close to them but their paths criss-crossed his memory, the trails of their scents, their calls and chirps, the hoarse howls of the invisible one who was sometimes down on the lake.

By now he knew he must never stop guarding the food spot. Sounds penetrated his deepest sleep, making him raise his nose to pick up a scent from the marsh. He fell asleep again but slept uneasily. His puppy sleep had been heavy; he had given himself up to it, abandoning any claim to the life that had satisfied him, until he woke up eager for warmth and a full stomach. Now his sleep was tattered and ragged, with sharp, easily awakened hunger, with alarm and muffled excitement, with sudden readiness that instantly flooded his primed muscles with coursing blood. Sleep and calm returned to him when it was quiet again or when the tantalising smell had drifted away.

Sleep and calm came from a full belly and the warmth of the sun, absorbed by his healthy, dry fur. But even then he was waiting.

He didn't have an image or a name for what he was expecting. But he would recognise it when he heard it or caught its familiar scent. He lived in wait like the lumpfish living in the cold, cloudy, turgid water of the stream underneath the ridges and rough patches in the ice.

One night he was awakened by a sound so familiar it called forth an image in him: bones cracking between powerful jaws. He pulled himself out of the hole and sat rigidly attentive under the spruce. The teeth went on crunching bones. He waited for a scent to complete the image, turning the crunching into his mother's teeth and the shadow down in the marsh into his mother. The moon was out and the crust of snow was gleaming. Branches cast a pattern on the white surface. He took a few steps across the expanse of crust and emerged from the shadow of the spruce. Now he could see the shape over by his food. He wanted it to be her, and his memory stretched and twisted to turn this long, thin

back and the far too bristly tail into his mother. On the verge of terror, he took small, cautious steps until he couldn't make himself go on. He was torn between vigilance and anticipation. Then he started off again, and what propelled him along the last stretch was sheer longing. But when he got close enough to see the long, thin legs, the triangular head with the long snout and pointed ears, he stiffened and stood still. The blood froze in his belly, bringing on waves of nausea. Terror made his fur rise. He saw eyes gleaming in the moonlight, reflected on the crust, and the look in them was alien and hostile. Now he caught the scent of fox.

He wanted to turn tail and flee back to his hole. But between the paws of the fox was a piece of the moose meat. When that smell reached him he had the urge to run up and bare his teeth. The fox didn't move. It stood still, a full-grown male with thick winter coat and bushy tail, every hair on end, filling a large space in the moonlight. A large space, a large body, he emitted wave after wave of pungent presence without moving.

The dog sat down. He sat suddenly and clumsily as if plopping his backside down on the kitchen linoleum. He lifted one back paw and began scratching his ear. He scratched and scratched as if he didn't have a care in the world other than his madly itchy ear. And the fox, mouth still open and upper lip pulled back, withdrew into the undergrowth. There he stood still and the pup continued scratching, his paw thumping the hard snow. The fox slipped away and was gone, reappearing down on the marsh: a back, a long tail, a vanishing streak.

The pup didn't know how he'd managed to get the fox away from his food. But the fox was gone and now he walked stiffly, sniffing its tracks. He left a few drops of urine here and there. This was the first time he peed standing up with one hind leg raised. Then he gnawed at the rib bone the fox had pulled out of the snow.

When he had finished he sat listening for sounds in the bright night. Then he started to bark. The sound rang out between the trees, high-pitched and tentative. He listened to the echo and barked again. Finally he was overcome by sleepiness and loped back in his own tracks to the hole.

★

The hoarse howls from off the lake often woke him at night. His body tensed and he growled. As he drifted back to sleep his throat and lungs would sometimes let out an instinctive, involuntary response. His own howling woke him up. He sat up straight and threw his head back, baring his throat. He bayed. At the tip of his muzzle his lips formed a small, round opening through which he pressed the air.

He walked on the crust of the snow now. His paws were still large and clumsy but his legs had grown longer. He flew forward. Now and then he stopped, listening for the hoarse cries from the lake. Behind him there were no longer any memories.

From the pasture in front of the cabin he could see the lake. The frozen surface reflected the moonlight. The ice was like a smooth bluish film extending into the distance, farther than he could see. His paws took him running. Out on the smooth surface his body grew light. He fell into a rapid, rhythmic stride and, after a while, a sprint. He was running for no reason, towards nothing. The moonlight and the cold and the speed made his body sing. There was no limit, no forest, no shore. On its own his body ran in loops, making a long, flat figure of eight on the bright surface. He didn't stop. His pace slowed by itself; the loops became smaller. Finally he was back at a lope, which was when he

felt the pain in his paws. He stopped and licked them. There was a salty taste he didn't recognise. The saltiness left a powerful scent in the snow.

The speed and the running of a moment ago were forgotten. He crossed the ice, following the sharp scent of fox. Sometimes there was another smell, dense, heavy and oppressive. It awakened memories but he had nothing to attach them to. He circled the holes drilled in the ice, sniffing around, pawing at the crust. He found wads of snuff and orange peel. His nose poked at them just as his memory did. When they were in his mouth he snorted, and the strong, nasty smell made him drop them again. Eventually he found a little burbot by a hole. It was frozen stiff but when his teeth sank into its back he tasted fish. He gobbled it up without even spitting out the head, licking his paws thoroughly afterwards.

He wanted to get back to shore but his own tracks went in so many different directions he was unable to follow them. They just led in circles on the ice. After a while he looked up, then headed straight for the rocks at the shoreline. Halfway there he thought he saw something crouching, lurking among the boulders, watching him. He turned off in a different direction. Once he was a bit farther away the lurking body disappeared, became a rock among the other rocks.

The moon was setting as he made his way back to the wooded area above the marsh. It was dark among the spruces and the snow wouldn't support his weight. Time after time he sank through until he finally curled up by a root, licking the salty tang of blood from his paws. The woods were just coming to life as he fell asleep. At dawn one bird after another warbled tentatively in the dense, moist air. But he was sleeping.

The meltwater made the forest hum. It gurgled under the snow. His paws sank into the slush. His belly was wet most of the time, and as soon as he had pulled himself up on a stump or found shelter by a fallen tree he would lick himself until his belly and paws were dry. The singing of the birds and the dripping of the water filled his ears. The bright light from above caught in his eyes and made him drowsy. Sometimes he tried lying on his side and sleeping in the sun, but he couldn't. The wetness always overtook him.

He was hungry. That night, after running on the ice, he had looked for his food spot at the edge of the marsh, but hadn't found it. By morning, after he had slept fitfully against a rock or the trunk of a spruce tree, the clear memory of the food spot had faded. Now all that was left was apprehension and hunger. He was nothing but an aching belly and plodding paws in the slushy snow. He had to lift his legs high to make any progress at all. The woods were full of clear scents and voices but he couldn't catch things that moved. He found frozen lingonberries in the melting snow by tree stumps.

In his sleep during the long, light mornings when the surge swelled in the forest, a sound reached him that he'd never heard before. It was a burbling like the murmur of rising water. He raised his head and listened, but fell asleep again when the waves of sound receded. One morning when he awakened the sound was so close he could discern voices in the murmuring. He stood up and started walking cautiously, his legs stiff with cold. There were rays of sunlight between the trunks of the spruces on the slope. He avoided it because of the glare. The gurgling song was now very close by. He could hear individual voices rising and falling. One disappeared and another bubbled up, rang in his ears for a long time and vanished into the murmuring. In front of

28

him was a little tarn, glimmering white with untouched snow.

Now the sun had risen above the spruce-covered slope. The surface of the tarn blinded him. But he could still see dark shadows moving down by the shore. When he started running he could hear a bird take flight and at once the rippling song went silent. For quite a while he nosed around on the ice, following the fresh scent. The only thing he found was a feather, a black curved feather from the tail fan of a large black grouse cock.

He roamed and he slept. In the early morning he was awakened again by the same song filling the forest. This time he crept more stealthily, keeping his belly to the snow when he paused to listen. It was murky and grey under the spruces. But he saw two round shadowy bodies pull apart, dancing towards each other and away again at the edge of the marsh.

It was as if they had arisen from the very murmur of voices and become solid and black. They were running with outspread wings, dragging their tails. He could hear them burble and gurgle. A bit farther away he could see more of them. The whole area was alive and moving, full of circling black bodies. The song rose and fell with their movements against the snow. He lay near them until the sun was in his eyes and the glare off their white tail feathers was blinding. He pounced, but only half-heartedly. The grouse cocks flew up. Heavy bodies with noisily flapping wings went off in so many directions his eyes couldn't follow a single one. He never saw the hens. They had scurried off into the reeds. He only heard their terrified cackling. As soon as the grouse had flown off he started scratching his ear.

★

Slushy water and sour lingonberries. Feathers in the moss, straggly, odourless. Nothing but water in his aching stomach, wet paws in the marsh. Push on, push on, slow and soggy. Chew on feathers, suck on bones. Water dripping on nose, stinging eyes and aching belly. Traipse and trudge. Crouch with belly to the snow. Push on with nose to the ground.

Odourless water. Meltwater. Hungerwater.

The moon creeps up on the forest. The night is not silent. It purls and ripples, it twitters and rustles. Up, keep going across the patchy ground. Body uneasy, forest uneasy. Patches of moonlight and snow, patches of shadow and dark marshland.

Sharp branches, paws and claws. Crouching stumps with furry backs and ears. Sleeping boulders. Fall asleep on damp lichen, frozen stiff and dizzy. Spots before the eyes. Hunger pangs and dull fear. Sleep it off. Sleep in the sun. Suck the warm teats. Doze off. Suck. Suck the warmth.

*

He came to a spot he recognised. It wasn't just one of the countless places where he caught a whiff of the restless phantom that was everywhere, his own scent. The silhouette of the grey building was familiar. He walked up to it, discovering the smell of his own urine on the wood of the door.

The barn door had rotted off its hinges and stood leaning against the entrance, forming an opening that was wider towards the bottom. He sniffed at it for a long time before he dared wriggle through. An unfamiliar smell, sharp and concentrated, bewildered him. Once inside he could see almost nothing. When he sniffed at the rough floorboards the dust made him sneeze. Something was hanging on the wall and he started chewing. It was stiff but his saliva softened it and the taste filled his mouth. He pulled off a piece and swallowed it, but that only made his bellyache worse. When he knocked over a rusty bucket he panicked at the clatter, dropped the halter, ran to the entrance and wriggled out.

A short distance away the fear let up. He lay by a spruce, staring at the building. It was still familiar, beating like his own heart, a sickening pounding that pitched him between terror and reassurance. At dusk the building seemed larger. In the constant murmur of water all around him he heard things that weren't there: people's voices. His memory singled out strands in the weave of sounds that could have been voices. But they weren't. The murmuring continued but no one emerged from the ramshackle building. He withdrew, dejected, curling up against a windfallen tree with its dry, compressed mass of soil and roots rising towards the sky.

At dawn the crows awakened him. They were circling above the marsh, telling him the same thing they told each other: food! With a couple of bounds he was there and they immediately flew up. Now he was the one who frightened them. He stood over the food on long legs, tugging at the rotting, shaggy flank.

Everything here was familiar. He was back at his marsh. The moose carcass was still there, though all that was left was a decomposing hide over some ribs and a few scattered bones. He didn't find much nourishment but plenty of unfamiliar scents, trails that went in circles, and droppings. He marked the tree trunks with a few drops here and there and then lay down on the slope, gnawing greedily at a thighbone that still had a few sinews. His mouth was bleeding. His incisors were loose and the gums tender where new teeth were breaking through. His permanent front teeth had already come in.

★

At first hunger is a spur, making legs grow long and forcing nose to the ground. Then it becomes a whip, lashing out at sensitive ears with sounds, striking through a deep sleep. It releases scents that soon are lost. It gnaws and torments from deep inside an aching cavity. The body, with matted fur, legs that dash, claws that tear and scrape, is merely the shape hunger assumes. There's nothing else inside. Only hunger.

★

The porous snow melted away. The marsh water rose. The top layer of ice on the lake was gone. His paws sank into grey slush and he had to retreat to the rocky shore. One night a storm blew in, awakening him from the numbness of hunger. He tried to curl up again and sleep but was too exposed. His ears were pressed back by the wailing wind. He had to go and find a spot in the woods under a spruce. There he lay, listening as the howling in the air snapped off branches. At dawn the wind was still strong, and fallen twigs and needles covered the snow under the trees. All smells had vanished from the world.

In the morning he faced the wind, angling down to the lake. Standing in the trees along the shore he was suddenly afraid. Massive grey shapes rose up and broke on the rocks. The churning waves boomed as they pounded against ice and stones. He didn't recognise this roiling, crashing lake with its black water and chunks of ice, and he retreated into the forest.

Keep going, keep going.

That was the day he found a dead vole. Its belly was swollen and it had yellow, protruding teeth. He turned it over with his paw and nudged it with his nose. The distended skin ruptured and a mess of liquid poured out. He left it at the foot of a spruce, covering it with leaves and needles. He roamed on, but for shorter and shorter stretches. Hunger ruled him in a different way than before. It made him dizzy and dazed. He longed for sleep, and if it hadn't been for the moisture, the clammy, dripping water that always soaked through the fur on his belly, he'd have slept for eternity.

★

If you found warm eggs among tufts of grass you would look around for birds. But if no one had told you where eggs came from you would crack them open and eat them, and when you were full you'd puzzle it out. You would look at the sun and the shiny yolks inside the shells you'd crushed and suppose the sun had laid them like roe in the grass and was now warming them until they were ripe.

The dog found them but didn't wonder where they came from, though he soon realised they had something to do with the sharp cries of the birds. He ate with his muzzle pressed into the grass, lapping the viscous whites with his tongue, slowly and thoroughly licking up the yolks, licking every blade of grass.

The last patch of snow on the marsh had vanished. In the forest there were scruffy drifts with hard, almost transparent crystals. The spruces had dropped their seeds and needles on them; the wind had brought down lichen and twigs.

The marsh was suffused with water. It flooded, forming two streams that ran down to the lake, murmuring and singing among the stones. In the forest and on the marsh, at the shore where birch and alder appeared in the opening beyond the blanket of spruce, on the point down towards the narrows, in the shallow bay, protected from the wind off the mountains in Norway – every day brought a shower of new voices. In the morning, when red and gold still lingered in the sky like gravel at the bottom of the brook, a shifting, quavering blanket of bird calls hung over the forest. Throats with yellow or rust-coloured or plain lava-grey patches were vibrating. Small bodies were filled with song. Though they were nothing but a handful of down, a few hollow bones and a mouthful of blood, their calls rang out. Their song rose like marsh water in the forest.

Wherever the sun dried and warmed the ground insects

were creeping and crawling. Early in the day the anthills slowly came to life. When the sun was highest in the sky the ants were at work repairing holes. If it was too cold in the morning the colony grew sluggish and didn't go out. The ants clung to each other, barely alive, so feeble that the anthill didn't even smell like piss when a paw scratched its rough surface.

But sunny days dominated. The sun warmed and incubated. It drew out bodies that had burned stored fat while sleeping. Hunger awakened in the forest. The voles started scurrying in the dry grass, looking for seed pods left from the previous autumn, for frozen lingonberries, cocoons and eggs.

At night the water in pit holes froze in thin sheets, injuring paws that broke through. The brown grass acquired a new film of ice. But the light came early. Before the ball of sun had emerged above the treetops in its haze of red, the entire forest was suffused with light.

Water and light rose in veins and stalks, in vessels and nerves and tiny roots. Voices were filled with light and light filled the warm eggs. It shot like sparks in newly awakened membranes and muscles filled with blood, pulsating inside the eggs.

He licked the light, sucked it. The water in the run-offs retreated. It was no longer the enemy; it was a bright voice under the stones. His belly was dry and he turned it towards the sun. He could have been killed in those moments of trust, lying there as if he'd suckled the sun, snoring in his puppy sleep. But though many were killed when winter hunger awakened in the forest, he was not among them.

★

All those living in dens and lairs around him had their own ways. From the moment daylight began filtering into their sleep until darkness fell and they tucked their beaks under their wings or curled their tails around their paws, each day was the same. They scurried up the same treetrunks and crept into the same holes. During the daylight hours they were constantly busy. Their world was familiar and they were on guard, for they all knew what was behind the tufts of grass and above the treetops, and what might be there.

During the long period of privation he'd wandered aim-lessly, his memory patchy, like clouds of damp fog. Sometimes he had run half-heartedly, without searching in earnest; sometimes he had fallen asleep by a treetrunk in the midst of chasing something that rustled or squeaked. Now he searched eagerly but knew where he was, even when a snapping twig or a faint rustle in the dry grass woke him from a nap.

He'd become wary of his old sleeping place on the slope by the marsh. Now he preferred the large spruces where the lowest layer of dark, needle-covered branches skirted the ground. But he never slept many nights in the same spot. After a while he would become uneasy. Sniffing around the place he'd slept, he wasn't sure what scents he picked up. Then he retreated, found another spruce or another pile of stones to crawl into. But he often returned to the old places that felt familiar, where he was on guard but not agitated. If too many indistinct trails of scent surrounded the spot he became confused, at worst afraid. But fear didn't strike often. He didn't know what brought it on. Fear stung; fear struck in the dark.

In the mornings his body was stiff and he had to stretch his numb legs again and again before the blood got moving and his joints loosened up. The sharp smells of early morning made him alert. Whatever had taken place in the grass and the moss had just happened. There were no lingering traces of creatures that by now were far away. He always began by scouring the marsh where he'd first found eggs. Searching was futile now, but the delicious, flavourful eggs remained with him. He had to forage in the marsh before he did anything else.

Every day he roamed the same area. The recent past hung in the air as wisps and trails. In the present, branches snapped; there was rustling, squeaking and scraping. But some things had happened so long ago that their smells had completely vanished. There were many such things. They happened once again when he reached the place where the scent had faded away. But now they happened inside him, with a jolt that made his muscles tense. He started searching, his snout rooting, his paws tearing at the ground.

Under the roof of the cabin, against the timbered wall where the ground was dry, there had been a dead magpie one morning. He couldn't walk past the cabin without investigating that strip of dry ground. When he crossed the pasture and came down to the wooded area on the point there was a rotting tree trunk that roused his excitement. This was the place he'd found large cocoons. He scratched at the reddish wood; it crumbled under his claws. There were no more cocoons, but that was where it had happened, and when he came across the trunk it happened again. Each time it grew fainter until eventually it sank into the ground and disappeared. Other things happened that made him watchful and momentarily roused, nose to the ground and ears pricked. If they brought more than a mouthful to eat, if they filled his belly, these things, too, would remain with him a long time.

★

The birch buds swelled and grew sticky. On the slope down to the inlet the sallow bushes were in bloom, covered with pollen and bright in the sunshine. He was alarmed the first time he saw them, thinking for a moment that they were large, luminous bodies.

Under the alders, pointed blades of grass, green and with an intense taste, were pushing up from beneath the grey-brown blanket of last year's leaves. There was a stand of nettles by the old manure pile at the barn; the air around them had a sharp smell.

The ground, too, was always changing. The pattern of wet areas and grass, of sounds and smells, shifted beneath him. Down by the shore the ground ended: no grass or tracks, just stones and the murmuring and lapping of the water. When the wind blew hard, pieces of wood washed up, scrubbed and polished by the smooth stones. The wood was shiny, pale and strange. The strip between the deep, constantly churning water and the wet ground where grass had taken root was a dangerous, rewarding borderland where creatures were left behind, with straggly, drenched feathers or soggy fur.

He always stayed as far as possible from the water's edge, stretching his neck towards the smells and setting his paws down cautiously. Along the shore there were no bushes. Though this made him uneasy, he often took the risk of letting himself be seen. Down there he always found something to eat.

If he went far out on the point he came very close to the other world. He could see the opposite shore and sometimes he heard dogs barking. He didn't dare go to the very tip. He was afraid of the other side. When he heard barking he wanted to howl, but fear stopped him. He crouched low in

clumps of brush on the bank, squinting in the wind, catching scents from the dangerous side.

From the shore that was usually sheltered from the wind he could hear the loud roar of the rapids. He couldn't see them and didn't know what they were. The water danced in eddies down towards the noise. It was dangerous out on the point. The surging of the water made him deaf. He couldn't hear sounds from the forest. He kept to the wetlands and took small, cautious steps on decaying logs. Only rarely did curiosity lure him out into the roar of the rapids.

Once he saw the silhouette of a long, arched back on the rocks in the narrows. It slid into the water and emerged on the opposite side. He saw the back lengthen into a tail, saw the undulating movement of the otter's leap to its den on the bank, but with his poor vision he lost track of the movement among the crowberry brush, and when he didn't pick up a scent he forgot about it.

On the shore by the inlet, beavers had felled birches and aspens, stripping bark and twigs from the trunks. The logs plunged into the water, naked and pale. He became familiar with the scent of beaver although he never caught sight of them. The ground was muddy and rough where the beavers had been at work so he kept to the woods. He didn't like mud sticking to his fur. He didn't like unnecessary trouble. Climbing tired him out and made him forget to listen and stay on guard. He was no longer a pup who acted carelessly, without considering. He'd become deliberate and cautious.

The path from the boat landing was overgrown; young spruce trees and birch saplings were so close together that he had a hard time making his way through. There was a murmur of bird sounds in there, rustling wings, shadows, blinking eyes. He never paid any attention to the little ones. They fluttered up on tiny, quick wings and vanished into the darkness of the enormous spruces. When he found one of them on the ground with ruffled feathers and limp neck he didn't connect it with the ones who fluttered and chirped. They were nothing to him when they were in the air; they were too quick. But the ones with heavy bodies that had a hard time taking flight, the flapping and squawking ones, those interested him. Where he picked up their scent he might find eggs.

The old summer pasture had a dense layer of last year's vegetation, brown and compacted by the snow. Now green blades of grass were lifting it up. From the warm space between the ground and the tip of the blades came the rustling of quick paws. He made his way slowly up the slope, his muzzle in the warm, fragrant mat, eating insects methodically while continuing to listen for the rustling. Down there he could smell vole.

Around the barn were stands of nettles. Those he avoided. To reach the marsh he had to cross an overgrown hollow bisected by a black, muddy ditch, where there was often a strong scent of moose.

He was quite familiar with the little marsh and its sparse, waterlogged pines. There, and along the shore, were his best fields. A narrow, wooded ridge extended into the grassy area of the marsh. His first sleeping place had been up there but he went no farther than the top of the ridge, where there was a sharp plunge towards an area he hadn't explored. On the incline the enormous spruces were so old and so dense that the ground under them was brown with needles. Nothing grew there.

In the cleared area above the cabin were the hares. He didn't go very far in that direction either. That was the end of the world as he knew it, the border between the clearing and the marsh. Whenever he ventured into the unknown he was very much on edge.

★

The ragged cover of grass and compressed leaves was in motion, lifted from below, bursting with new growth. From the space beneath the roof of grass came the buzzing and whirring of insects, but there were voles down there as well. He often stood still, head lowered, ears cocked, listening.

One morning he heard a faint peeping. It sounded like birds under the grass. Following it with his ears, he found it was louder by the large rock near the cabin steps. The scent grew more intense in the clumps of grass. When he clawed at them the muffled peeping stopped. He clawed again and found hairless bodies, the smell of blood. He didn't look, just gobbled.

The vole nest was full of young. He didn't chew until he got to the last one. The nest – tangled tufts of grass – lay between his paws. He put his cheek to the warm ground, his jaws crunching. The blood, the warmth, the spasms spurred him, making him eat faster than he ever had before. Only later did he feel the warmth and the pleasure, coursing in indolent waves through his hard, sinewy body.

He found a dry spot on the slope and stretched his legs and paws. His belly made swishing and gurgling noises as it digested. Lying with eyes half closed, he felt shivers of satisfaction, pleasure and warmth. His paws twitched in his sleep and his upper lip drew back from his teeth. He was hunting.

★

The sun hatched many eggs on long stems. They swayed in the wind off the mountains. He nipped at them when he crossed the wet ground by the shore. That wind was just fresh sky and water. It could continue for many days in a row, caressing the hardy yellow flower heads as they swayed and bobbed. The rowans had unfolded their leaves in long points like bird claws, white side up in the breeze. The wind sang in the birch leaves.

The wind off the mountains never bothered him. It never brought anything stinging or sticky, nothing worrisome or threatening like the capricious wind that sometimes blew the water in the rapids back against the flow. The wind off the mountains was steady. Sometimes it picked up and then the lake showed its white fangs off in the distance. High above, the wind sang in the spruces. In the grass it was warm. The creatures that rustled and squeaked weren't affected by the wind, even when it made enormous waves in the grass.

The wind raised the fur on his back but his muzzle was down among the voles. The grass was so full of strong smells that he sometimes had to raise his head to clear his nose. It smelled of yarrow about to bloom, a compact, heavily spicy scent. The mouldering humus was steaming, crawling with blind, hard-shelled insects that ground their teeth, criss-crossed by fat, industrious bugs the thrushes could find by listening. He himself caught them only by chance when his sharp claws scratched the ground. The delicate scents of cranesbill, cow parsley, buttercup, snakeweed and the slender, hardy bluebell, sheep's sorrel and tormentil were intermingled with that of the grass. The hoverflies and wasps and the fuzzy bumblebees filled the world that was the flowering roof of the pasture with a slowly rising and falling hum.

The dog ploughed through the grass, leaving deep furrows behind him. Sometimes when the sun, the scents and the sounds made him dizzy with languid pleasure, a delight so sweet it almost tickled, he lay belly up, rubbing his back against the grassy carpet. He wriggled, his body coiling, front paws waving. Afterwards he got up quickly and shook his coat. When he ambled off he was himself again, composed and on guard. Behind him the grass was flattened and the thin blades of cranesbill and starwort were pressed down. Vessels had been broken, green blood was flowing. Slowly the work began to restore everything to its pre-disaster state. Fluids found their way to vessels that didn't leak. Wounds dried up and blisters healed. By then, though, he was already lying on a rock near the shore, licking his coat clean from everything that had stuck to it in the sea of grass.

★

At night the large grey creatures emerged. They were often standing down where the forest met the marsh. In the stillness they resembled rocks and shadows, heavy shapes that dissolved in the dark and seemed to disperse among the tree trunks. His ears and nose told him where they were but his eyes could no longer make them out.

Resting in his old sleeping place, he became accustomed

to them. Their movements were slow and imposing and they made careless noises, breaking twigs and tramping through mud with their hooves. They made wheezing sounds and the bark ripped in their powerful teeth. He saw their legs moving, white in the dim light. They were always together. It was quite a while before he realised there were two of them. If one appeared at the edge of the marsh in the erratic dawn rays flickering before his eyes, if the shadows and the sound of snapping twigs coalesced into a single body, then he knew there would be another one down there too. He listened, one ear cocked, for the one who was missing.

But he didn't know they were yearlings, or that the female moose who had given birth to them and nursed them last year was the carcass that had kept him alive from late winter to spring. The hunters had sent the dogs after her but she got away. She'd survived till midwinter with a shattered jaw, and had died of starvation.

★

His nose was honed in on voles and mice and the concentrated smell of bird nests; he ignored most of what the ground and grass could tell him. There was a blur of smells everywhere.

But he followed the tracks of the moose. Plunging into the fresh trails they made gave him intense pleasure. His entire body quivered in a frenzy of joy. But when he picked up their scent he stopped. He could hear them wheezing. A yelp forced its way out of his throat, confusing him, and he pulled back.

Restlessness came over him. All the creatures living in dens and holes, moving about in the pale light under the trees, creating new wafts of scent in the night, all of them had their own ways. Only he walked with his nose to the ground, searching and listening, waiting. When he'd found a mouthful that relieved the pangs of hunger he looked for a place to sleep, but he was always expectant.

No one came. His restlessness stirred as the light faded. It became intense when the smell of moose in the tracks merged with their scent in the air. Bewildered, he withdrew under a spruce, licking his paws and listening. It seemed as if each and every creature around him had scents and trails that were their own and he was the only one searching for a way to make sense of a jumble of sounds and restless shadows.

But he didn't find it. He could find no trace of the pack he'd once belonged to.

He was on his own, working out what he needed to know. A short-eared owl had swiped him across the face with the side of her wing. He'd thought it was a game bird when he heard the swoosh, but game birds fled, flapping off between the trees, not even attacking in self-defence. Owls, though, dived down. From that day on he listened for that swooshing noise, distinct from the sound of game birds.

One morning as he was standing at the water's edge, nosing around for fish the otter had left, the stones shifted. When he tried to pull himself up one of his hind legs was caught. It was a long time before he managed to free himself, and then only with great effort and intense pain.

The soreness stayed with him. The collapse of the stones was a longer-lasting lesson than the reprimand of the owl. He walked on three legs, hobbling and hopping when he had to. During this period his corkscrew tail was often limp. He didn't go lame, but when the wound healed he had a bump on his hock that he often licked. When the mornings were cold and rainy the pain reawakened. He grew accustomed to it. The pain became part of him, just like the bump.

He knew what to expect from the owl. When she plunged, gliding on outspread wings, he should keep out of the way. The owl and the stones.

There were other things that didn't reveal themselves. He no longer ambled along as he'd done as a pup, absent-minded and eager. He crossed open spaces quickly, hunching down, his entire body tense from listening. When the summer heat hung over the pasture and the murmur of bird calls died out towards morning, he was a thin, muscular dog who often stood by a birch or a rowan, letting the shadow of the leaves play across his dark mask and slanted eyes as if he were aware of them and wanted to conceal them so they wouldn't give him away. He avoided the rustling aspens, which interfered with listening, and he avoided the side of the point near the rapids except for an occasional early morning foray to sniff for fish scraps.

More and more often, he followed the trail of the moose. It served no purpose but felt compelling. His eagerness had no direction, no goal, and always left him bewildered. But the scent took him farther and farther from the little world near the cabin that he knew so well: the marsh, the pasture, the point. He found his way to other marshes, to rocky terrain covered with bog moss, dark forests with wood grouse, swampy shores of dark, unfamiliar lakes. Above him a buzzard screeched.

He always caused a commotion. Birds flew up in front of him with piercing shrieks that went on for a long, long time. That could mean eggs. He searched, nose to the grass, letting the shrieks guide him. When they grew loud and anguished he was close, when they died out he'd lost the trail.

Now there were bodies inside the eggs. Most of the time, though, only the shells were left; the warm, moist contents were gone. He wasn't interested in the shells. The young that had hatched by the shore fled to safety in the water, leaving tiny rippling wakes on the smooth surface. He tested the wetness with his paw but didn't like it. Once he'd plunged in after them, but when his paws no longer touched bottom he couldn't see across the water. He paddled, but no matter how far he stretched his neck he didn't catch sight of anything alive, so he turned back to land, shook himself thoroughly and loped off without looking back.

While following the moose trail, he'd come across a body of water not far from the marsh. He began including it in his daily rounds. Each time he went there and walked around the shore he was less tense and hunched down.

It was a tarn, black and almost round, quite near the big lake. A brook made its way down through the dense forest of old spruce, bringing water from the tarn to the larger lake, an inland sea with cold, restless blue water that never was silent.

The beavers had made a dam in the brook. Along the far bank the spruces and small pines were turning yellow. On his side the banks were steeper. Though the soil was full of passageways the ground held; water hadn't reached the roots of the trees and they were still healthy. In the passageways the scent of beaver was strong.

In the evening the steep side was sunny and he lay there in a dense thicket of crowberry brush and bilberry, letting the warmth sink into his fur. If he lay still for a long time he sometimes caught sight of a beaver's head gleaming in the light, cutting straight through the water. He always followed the beavers with his gaze but didn't move or become agitated. It was impossible to get near them.

By the passageways along the banks where the beavers came ashore there was nothing for him. He picked up their particular scent and the smell of their droppings. There were no fish scraps, not a single feather, either, but they left stripped branches everywhere.

The loud splash of a large, flat tail sometimes awakened him. He liked lying there listening to them. The sound of their gnawing could be heard from far off. When they thought they were alone they poked around on the shore. They were clumsy on land. He couldn't see them, but he could hear their heavy bodies and the twigs that snapped in their jaws.

The sun was low in the sky. It was no longer warm but stung in his eyes as it played among the trunks of the spruces. He liked lying there listening to sounds that signalled neither flight nor a threat. He and the beavers had nothing to do with each other, but they were there, in the same evening sun, by the same dark water that glowed in its reflection. He liked the sounds they made, their company.

★

A vole in the grass. He heard it a moment ago. He recognises the sound of the hindquarters, heavy and sliding. It's not the scampering of a mouse.

He's standing tense, head lowered. His ears are cocked forward, the cartilage stiff, the hairs raised.

They're both stock-still now, but as soon as the vole at his feet moves, he'll pounce. Down there is the warm world of the grass with its whirring and humming, but he's only listening for one distinct sound: the vole. It's there somewhere, blinking, its heart pumping blood, listening, every hair in its grey-brown fur on end.

The dog remains still so he won't lose the scent. The wind off the lake blows through the meadowgrass; the pasture billows and shimmers, blinding him. But he doesn't move. In the jumble of sounds under and above him there's only one sound he's waiting for.

He never tires. A vole that's not threatened moves straight through the grass, perhaps towards its nest. It may freeze warily in its tracks but will start moving again. The dog often misses when he tries pouncing in the cover of grass, but his ears never lose track of a vole that has come to a halt somewhere beneath him among the coarse stalks of wolfsbane.

Now. A faint sliding. The cow parsley doesn't move, but that's where it came from. The dog is poised for the strike. His nose and front legs dive into the grass. He's got it, but only for a moment. Frenzied wriggling under his front paws. Then it scurries between his legs. Two more tries. It's injured and can't get away. Now he bites and the tiny, warm body goes limp between his jaws.

He takes it with him out of the grass, lying down under a spruce at the edge of the forest. With his paws he pins the vole against a root, tearing at it with his front teeth until the fur rips open.

He's not especially hungry. The pasture is full of voles and he's become skilled at finding them, though he's still somewhat clumsy when he pounces. But after a few hours of hunting in the morning he's no longer so eager that he gobbles them up right away. He carries off his prey, tears at the fur for a long time, leaves bits and pieces.

The strong wind blowing off the lake creates a little tempest in the crown of the spruce. The sound makes him sleepy. He dozes, eyelids heavy. The pasture rustles in the wind and blades of grass gleam when it combs them apart. The tiny birch leaves shimmer, too, catching the sun. Birch saplings sprout up here and there in the heavy grass, an invasion from the forest.

White flecks swirl across his field of vision. He knows what they are. Butterflies don't have much taste. Bumblebees sting in your mouth. He knows.

In his drowsiness he gazes out across the familiar pasture. The grey fluttering of birds. The flecks of butterflies. The grass is fragrant and the air is filled with pollen.

In the mornings he sees the vixen. She's usually there before he is, hunting for voles, surrounded by a haze of powerful scent. If he rushes her she vanishes, running low in the grass, which closes above her.

They've never approached each other but he's lain on a hill above the inlet, looking down on her den. Her cubs often come out in the sun. Growling, they squabble over bird wings. Though there are sometimes food scraps outside the den he never goes down there. There's something between the foxes and him, something that keeps them apart.

The pasture is his. It billows under his drowsy gaze, humming and whirring.

★

Catching the young hare brought about a change in him. So much blood and warmth at once. Such extended pleasure, along with the lingering sense of surprise.

KERSTIN EKMAN

It had happened quickly. The hare popped up in the grass, rustling in a clump of ferns. With a single leap he had him; the smell of blood merged with the smell of broken ferns. The rustling of stiff fronds and their bittersweet fragrance excited him long afterwards.

The full-grown hares kept their distance. Not so long ago he'd thought of them as huge. As a pup he'd kept still by the root of a spruce when they bounded by on the crust of the snow. He hadn't felt safe.

It was the same with the large birds, the black or brown-speckled ones that flapped up from the thicket. For a long time he didn't dare hunt them, remembering the hard wing of the owl, the reprimand in his own pasture.

But now there were others like those hares, only smaller and more afraid. The fine hairs of fur so erect the downy undercoat caught the light. The eye. The smell of death even before his fangs sank in. The stench of terror.

Prey.

There were wood grouse chicks in the grass. Cheeping, scurrying in the same glassy-eyed terror of being caught.

The dog was changing, growing into his muscular body. Inside him, something was evolving: a purpose. Filling his mouth with blood and warmth, keeping it filled. Pouncing when he heard a rustling noise. Sinking in his fangs. What was there to be afraid of in the shadows? His body was nearly full grown now. It hardened around this awareness: can strike. Am stronger than the rustling and the shadows.

★

The warm nights brought gnats and black flies. They plagued him and he never got used to it; the torment didn't become part of him. He tried to flee but there was nowhere the insects didn't catch up with him. The flies crept into his eyes, the gnats settled in his belly fur. He licked the swellings they left. Only the wind brought relief.

The voices were also part of the warm nights. He avoided them. Now he was sleeping up in the woods, on windy mountain slopes where the gnats and flies were swept away, but the unfamiliar terrain made him uneasy. The wind was blowing too hard for him to hear properly. He was on edge.

In the mornings, when he came down to the pasture to hunt, the voices were gone. The smell of smoke hung in the air. Gusts of wind brought other enticing smells, thick and

unfamiliar. He began going down to the shore and searching. There was fish blood on the stones. If he got there
before the vixen he might come across a tiny, stiff fish that
had been left. He found rubbery sausage skins. Although
they were salty and hard to chew, he couldn't resist them. He
was thirsty after going through the scraps the fishermen had
left by the cold campfire, and his mouth burned. He lay at
the edge of the lake by the boat landing, licking his paws
clean from grease and soot. Then he took a long drink of
cold lake water.

★

From the bramble down by the shore a surge of living
creatures makes its way toward the pasture. The air is humming and sticks in his throat when he breathes. Everything
warm-blooded is fair game. There are swellings on his hide
from the stings. The more he licks the more it burns. He
wants to escape to a cool breeze, but the wind has completely died down. During the white nights of summer the
water is smooth.

He spends his days stretched out motionless under a

spruce, as close to the water as he can get without being seen. There are often boats on the lake now. The voices make him uneasy. He wants to get away from them but the heat in the clearing is so intense he's forced to turn back. There's no escaping them by the shore; the voices even punctuate the night.

He hunts in the early morning when there's still a trace of cool night air, going down to the lake to drink while it's still quiet along the shore. The goldeneyes dive for food, pulling up strips of vegetation that quiver on the smooth surface. He listens for the sound of the beavers.

Everything is familiar. He hears the same sounds he always does, but beyond them are the voices. They're present even when they can't be heard. The activity along the shore has scared off the otter and her young. Their scent gradually fades away. The fox enters their den and roots around. Soon his own scent has wiped out every memory of the timid otters.

The shore belongs to those who dare to live with the voices of human beings. The dog is one of them, but he's on edge, his body tense from the plague of gnats and from listening. There's no restfulness in the light, warm nights, no deep sleep. In the pasture the valerian shines so brightly that the opaque bells of the flowers seem to contain a white light. The sickly smell reaches him in little bursts. Nothing is forgotten.

*

One morning he was out at the point, digging for mouse nests under the spruces. He let down his guard for a moment, not listening around him, attuned only to faint sounds under the moss. Then the voices swept over him. There was barking and a creaking noise. He heard a smack and water splashing, then wood scraping against stones. He was so close to the shore he could glimpse the boat and all the people in it through the alders.

They came ashore without noticing the dark mask in the speckled shadow of the alders, but he couldn't escape from the point. Their sharp voices and careless movements were all around the cabin. He crouched in the blueberry brush. No matter how hard he listened he wasn't sure where they were. They tramped around the pasture and slammed the cabin door. Windows flew open. Rugs and tablecloths snapped in the air. None of these noises were familiar. He was completely bewildered by them, lying with his head cocked, ears perked to pick up the sounds. Even if he'd been able to see what they were doing he couldn't have made sense of it. Axes chopping. The screech of a saw on wood. The clattering of a bucket. Last of all the smell of smoke pouring out.

Lying there in this chaos of sounds and insistent scents, he waited for a chance to get away, but the people were unpredictable. The smallest ones hollered and flattened the grass, throwing an object that kept landing near him. When they fetched it he could pick up their smells, which were very concentrated and seemed to burn and sting.

He withdrew farther out on the point. Although he was lying still, he was agitated. All other creatures were in motion at specific times. They hunted and searched and then they looked for a den or a branch. But the people at the cabin didn't leave, allowing him to sneak away. It was impossible to outwait them. When they'd been quiet for a few minutes the noise and activity started all over again, without warning or respite. Their chaos was between him and the forest. Each time they came in among the trees on the point he grew more terrified. He was prepared to defend himself.

Towards dawn he broke out. By then it had been calm for quite a while after the last one had returned from the fishing spots by the narrows and gone inside. The dog crossed his tracks in the damp grass when he fled.

Belly close to the ground, he followed the shore of the shallow inlet and then ran in among the scrubby birches by the pasture. Without bothering to look for the easiest path, he bounded across the wet area below the barn. It was covered with meadowsweet, which left a dense, honey-like smell when it broke off, making him dizzy. He ran through the marsh, black mud splattering around his legs. When he reached the spruce forest he had to slacken his pace. He loped along until exhaustion dulled the tension in his muscles. The memory faded. The throbbing sensation in his throat and lungs let up and his heartbeat grew steadier.

He was extremely thirsty; all day and all night he'd been too afraid to drink. As he started looking for water his body began to relax. Weariness came over him in the chill before dawn. He discovered a brook and drank for a long time. As he wound down he just lapped sporadically, standing with hanging head, letting the murmuring of the brook clear his head and drown out the loud surge of blood in his ears.

Then he pushed on through the forest. Dawn awakened all the creatures that had perched on twigs to sleep. There was a soft flutter quite nearby: the bold Siberian jays. He was accustomed to them and kept going.

Exhaustion made him increasingly sluggish and empty inside. Once the sun was up he came upon a boulder to rest by. The warmth of the sun found him there; it penetrated through his furry coat to his tired, tingling body. He slept in fits and starts while the warmth took over, healing and calming him. Only when the jays came too close did his paws twitch.

*

That day he didn't hunt. He didn't recognise the forest around him. He was searching, but not for food; it was familiar places he was after, and the smell of his own markings. He left no drops of urine, merely stayed on guard and kept on searching. He didn't empty his bladder until it was painfully full. Towards evening he started covering longer stretches at a time, loping at a steady pace, stopping once in a while to listen. But even the blend of sounds in the air had changed. Everything was different.

He headed uphill. Sharp rocks protruded and he had to climb. He was frightened of stones that might shift under his weight but he had to get across the rocky area. Inside him was a cavity that could only be filled by familiar things. No matter where he stopped, listening and sniffing, the wind brought only the unfamiliar, and it was vast.

The unfamiliar was hunger and stone. It was gravel and debris he'd never seen before, blasted-out strips of new logging roads, blotches of diesel oil in the gravel. It was rusty iron, plastic containers, mouldering cloth, beer bottles and jagged rocks. The pads of his paws got cut. Eventually he retreated from the strip; it had seemed easy to walk on but it exacted a price on his paws.

He drank from a brook, standing in the water for a long time. It soothed the pain in his paws. The running water cleared his nose but he still couldn't pick up any scents he recognised. The only relief from fear and confusion was to keep going.

The farther up he got the sharper the air became. The cleared area was huge. He tried to avoid piles of twigs and woodchips but there was no way round. Tractor ruts, deep as ditches, cut into the ground. Above him a buzzard sailed on outspread wings, screeching. It wanted him to leave. He would have been glad to escape the horrible noise and the circling overhead, but there was no forest to be found.

★

In the days that followed he could only hunt in the cleared area. The rough terrain made it difficult to find anything. Tracking prey was impossible. The buzzard could strike from the air but the dog had to make his way on the ground through brambles of brush and muddy tractor ruts.

Hunger made him clumsy and overexcited. He found a couple of mouse nests with litters of young. Once the ache in his belly let up he started listening for squeaks from the nests instead of the rustling of adult animals scurrying under the brush. He never caught enough to fill him up and make him sleepy. The constant hunger in his belly drove him on through lacerated terrain where the smell of diesel over-powered the scent trails he tried to follow.

The sun burned down on the cleared area during the day. He tried to find shade by the piles of brush. At first there had been water in the tractor ruts but it had dried up. Thirst drove him out into the heat. At midday the only sound was the monotonous buzzing of the horseflies, a dull song from no apparent source in the scorching air. The buzzard didn't appear at midday and the dog could roam without its screeching surveillance.

One night he walked a long way in the dim light, driven by thirst. Nose to the ground, he searched for moist patches but found only dryness and debris. Often he felt apprehensive, as if something were after him.

There was no wind to pick up a scent. He walked in loops, frequently twisting round to detect a pursuer. Hunger and thirst made his muscles tire easily. Sometimes he wanted to curl up by a boulder and let weariness overpower him, but the nagging sensation of having something on his trail drove him on.

When the darkness over the cleared area lifted at dawn and the piles of grey brush shifted to red again, he heard running water. He started off at a trot but remained on guard. Water in a brook rippled among stones. The air was different. Dawn had brought the sound of birds.

He reached the murmuring water, running across stones and the trunks of small, felled spruces, but he didn't dare stand in the open and drink. Pushing on to a place where the brook ran in a crevice between some rocks, he found a sheltered spot where he could lap the cold, sparkling water until the burning in his throat subsided. Then he listened. The wind had awakened, bringing bird calls and the fragrance of pine needles. The forest was close by. But the one whose presence he sensed was not discernible and there was no rustling.

He crept along the brook to find better protection before drinking his fill. He was now going upstream towards the smell of forest. Then the wind changed, bringing back his early-morning apprehension. It blew from the opposite direction through the brushwood by the brook and there was a loud crackling in the leaves. The dog caught the scent of predator. It stung in his nose.

He never saw her. She was resting on the boulder where he'd first stopped to drink. Eyes wide, she watched him crashing forward. The tufts in her ears quivered. Then she glided down and crossed the brook in the opposite direction. Her large cat pads left their marks in the damp sand of the brook.

When he got to the forest it didn't engulf him, just forced him on. He took the first hill in leaps and bounds. Large stands of blue sowthistle snapped. He heard birds flying up, shrieking. For a long time he ran along a ridge, hearing only the surge of blood in his ears.

Now the wind picked up, singing high above in the spruces. Surging wind, surging blood. No quiet. He was frantic. Forgetting was remote and the memory of the unfamiliar scent was near. It was the scent of a creature that attacked; his body knew that instinctively. Now he was running, but he wasn't following a trail. He ran to escape the memory, to forget.

★

The loon called out from above a distant lake. Up here the waters were cold. The loon's cry lingered in the air, a quivering ribbon of sound.

He sometimes returned there, to the steep, straight banks, but the intervals in between were long. He'd become a rambler, a rover.

There were no abandoned pastures this far up, no dense coverings of grass where voles rustled. Hunger drove him on. He covered long stretches each day. At first he had nothing to eat. He was dizzy and often had to rest.

Day by day he adapted to this new life, always on the move. He started finding wood grouse hens and their broods. He herded the frightened, peeping chicks, running rapidly in a wide circle where he'd heard the cackling and the hen taking flight. He grabbed each chick by the neck and chomped. The fluttering wings and twitching body excited him. His jaws clamped down again. His teeth ripped through feathers and down, reaching warm flesh.

He rarely caught game birds, surviving mainly on rodents. At the foot of the spruces he sniffed out mouse nests and tore out the young, but up here he never found very much in any one place. He loped on, a muscular grey body, almost invisible in the sheets of fog across the marsh at dawn.

Sometimes he crossed his own tracks, returning to places they'd disappeared, where only the scent of an old marking clung to a stump. This wasn't enough to make the place seem familiar. Only where the loons were: there he often stopped, lying on the steep northern banks above the tarn and listening. He rarely saw the loons, just their streaks in the water, but he heard their cries from far away as he roamed the ridges; that made him want to turn back.

★

He covered more ground than hunger compelled. When he was running long distances he had an economical, slightly uneven lope that didn't tire him out. It took him deep into a different area, into belts of forest in the mountains. Under high stands of blooming sowthistle he listened for lemmings. They were easy to catch: prey that went limp when he bit them across the back, revolting little bags of patchy skin. If he was hungry he swallowed them, otherwise he let them be. Some of them didn't run away; instead they sat on their haunches, chattering furiously. At first this bewildered, almost frightened him.

He ate cloudberries that had ripened in the sun. At dawn he sneaked up on game birds out on the marshes but he never caught anything in such open terrain. When he'd frightened them off he did as they did, gobbled wet cloud-berries until his belly felt heavy. He knew the foxes came here to eat. When he got farther up the mountainside he caught another scent that he avoided, of something heavy that made enormous, deep tracks in the marshy soil. This scent made him veer and get as far away as he could.

The marshes were narrow, running between the ridges and the islands of birch forest where the ground was dry. Up here the wind had more bite. Black-beard lichen fluttered in the birches and the lady fern and sowthistle rustled. There was rarely a period of calm between the gusts, and the wind from the mountains carried a whiff of snow.

One day he crossed the last of the marshes, coming up to a treeless slope. The ground was hard, covered with brush and heather. The wind pressed his ears back, making him uneasy. He could hear nothing but the whining in the air. When he scared up a grouse he was startled. It seemed to come out of nowhere, tearing at the air with its flapping wings. He started noticing rocks and thickets of dwarf birch and willow. He kept a lookout by them, crouched and lis-tening, but the grouse always came from unexpected directions and he could never catch them. Frustration made him more and more restless and irritable as he ran.

He came to a large field of snow that was trampled down by hooves and speckled with droppings. The snow was coarse, porous and sunken. He sniffed at reindeer hairs and ate some snow but was afraid to walk on the expanse of white. Disturbed by the roaring wind in his ears, which deafened him and made his surroundings unreliable, he turned and began loping downward.

That night he slept under one of the first large spruces he came to once he was back in the forest. The days had grown shorter and no insects tormented him, but he was stiff when he awakened in the morning and the bump on his hind hock hurt. Below him the marsh lay under a layer of frost. Each blade of grass was pristine and powdery when he started nosing for the sickly-sweet smell of overripe cloudberries.

*

He was heading down, running long stretches each day. The mountain wind at his back carried his own scent ahead, making it impossible to pick up whatever was moving or hiding in front of him, but he paid no attention since he wasn't hunting. He loped along unevenly and purposefully. His paws got used to the gravel of the logging roads. His pads became hard and slick, his claws dull and worn down.

He'd turned back just before the first night of frost when he encountered a sharp wind on the mountainside. Since then he'd only hunted at dawn. Even if he didn't catch anything he started running after a while. What drove him was a stronger incentive than hunger.

After drinking from a brook he would doze for a while under a spruce, but never for long. Soon he was on his way again. He didn't know where he was heading, but an inner sense told him he should run towards something more compelling than the cry of the loon above a distant mountain tarn.

★

Not all the days were strong, bold days for running. Confusion seized him sometimes, making him run aimlessly, not knowing if he was hunting or just following something distant he'd caught on the wind. When the rain washed the logging road clean from gravel and dug furrows in the sand he stayed off it.

Long, cold rains blew in off the ocean beyond the mountains. Clouds shrouded the jagged ridges in grey mist, not dissolving until they had emptied all their water over the forests and marshes. But the one caught in the downpour didn't know where it had come from or where it was going.

He was in a chamber of swirling water, trapped and miserable. His coat was drenched nearly down to the skin, a thick, unpleasant wetness that made him so cold he shivered all night no matter how tightly he curled up around himself. His hock ached.

When it wasn't raining too hard he would run anyway, at a measured, steady pace, a dark grey body with worn paws and a tight belly. He was running from the pain and his hunger and confusion, which pursued him like persistent, raw fog.

By day, the one who swooped down was in the spruce tree, dozing. The one who hunted voles was by the edge of the marsh. The little ones who cheeped and fluttered busied themselves in the trees. Each was where it belonged. They circled, roamed and fluttered, each in its own domain, and they always returned. But he was the one who kept running.

One night he slept near the logging road in a jumble of roots and stones. There were raspberry seeds between his teeth. He was engulfed in a freezing fog that muffled all sounds. He slept curled up, stiff from the cold.

At dawn the wind lifted the fog, carrying with it a complex fabric of smells that penetrated his sleep. His paws twitched and he started whimpering like a pup.

When he woke up he stood facing the wind, taking in the scents. It was all his. It was far more compelling than the cry of the loon. He took off running before he had even peed, before he had even found a stream to drink from.

He reached the marsh up above the pasture before the last clouds of mist had risen from the sedgegrass. The higher ground was orange after the frost, and the pit holes were black and saturated with rain. He sniffed. Everything was familiar. His paws knew every bump in the ground and nothing frightened him. His markings were still there in the wood of the barn. He peed on it again. It was all his, but he needed to mark it once more.

Although he was hungry he didn't feel like hunting. The

scent of a hare hung in the wet grass. It was quite fresh but he didn't follow it. He needed to ring in the whole area first. Nose to the ground, he ran in circles. Lots of others had been through this grass. The enormous grey creatures had left huge prints. They'd broken the stalks of meadowgrass and ploughed through the dark green blanket of leaves covering the wetlands, now starting to turn brown.

★

Everything that happens is inside him. It has already happened. Everything that happens is vivid within. He knows. It flares up, flashes like a wing in the dark night, settles again. It encompasses a life that has been lived.

Remembering and forgetting are the same murky depths. Something swirls up from the sludge – he recognises it. It settles – he forgets but knows. He is just the hard mask over vivid things remembered, elusive things forgotten.

He roams. A shape, grey fur and a black mask. White patch on the neck. Eye slits. He roams through wisps of memory, hovering over the soft brown sludge of oblivion.

The flutter of a wing, the flick of a sharp claw. He

crouches. Low to the ground, body taut, he sniffs from behind the mask.

Lake water laps the stones, gently and rhythmically. The yellow foam between water and stone contains the memory of long, habitual licking, a rhythmic, murmuring memory that will soon be effaced.

The pasture grass is dying back. Thick, rough stalks, brown spotted leaves; coarse vegetation prevails. Faded blue wolfsbane rustles in the wind near his ear. There's a sickly-sweet smell of decay from the dampness. The voles move slowly in the wet, heavy grass. The dog listens for their sounds.

His ears are alert and warm with blood. The cupped cartilage with its fine fur quivers. His hearing shifts from short to long distance, from what the wind carries to what is drawn into it. Ragged fragments of sound attach to the knowledge concealed deep within him.

Deep inside he has a core. It is his sun.

Throughout the spring and summer the cranesbill blossoms in the pastures, the wolfsbane, the quaking grass and the stitchwort flowers have all turned towards their sun. It sent water through them, drew up salt and nutrients. Their sun warmed them by day, putting them to sleep when it set.

But he carries his sun inside. He moves with it. Even in the dark of night it is there and it is what sends him out into the marsh and what allows him to keep roaming on frosty mornings, finding what he needs.

Late summer days arrived, bringing calm to the overgrown pasture. Many voices were gone. Every night of frost made the marsh a deeper yellow and the cloudberries more faded. The berries no beaks had found dropped away, into the mouldering humus.

Gusts blew in off the mountains, day after day, clearing the air. He felt the bite of the wind as he lay in the sun at the top of the rise behind the barn, squinting. The choppy waves on the lake were like fangs.

The voles in the marsh had grown so sluggish it was difficult for them to get away. He hunted up there most of the time now, in spite of all the noise he made ploughing through the meadowsweet. The wind whistled loudly in the spruces. He didn't know much about what was happening beyond the pasture. He was surrounded by noises that dulled his memory. But he avoided the point and the lakeshore.

There were frostbitten, scent-laden mornings when he could hear things far away. Sharp dog barks. Car doors slamming and engines revving.

One morning a rifle shot whined in the distance. He didn't understand it any more than he understood the sounds of the cars. It shattered the crisp air with its whizz. Again. And again. His ears buzzed for a long time.

By the time the wind had awakened the lake, making long, dark waves on the surface, he had forgotten the shots.

But there were more uneasy days. The sounds from the world on the other side of the rapids were sharper, more sudden. The dogs over there knew something.

Beyond his own marsh, in the dense, old forest where the wood grouse lived, and around the little bogs and the flat, rocky areas, the peace was also disturbed. Moose crossed the marshes on their way to higher ground. The pair of yearlings went farther and farther afield. He heard loud blaring, the trumpeting of the young bull moose. The female was being pursued by a bigger moose the grey dog never saw. This bull kicked up the ground and left his scent in the holes. The young female evaded him, running in long loops with the trumpeting young bull close behind, the big one never far away.

The dog listened in two directions. He didn't hunt much now, day or night. The skin on his belly was so tight his tendons showed. Often he stood still, head cocked, trying to make sense of the loud, unrecognisable noises. Hooves kicking wet moss off stones. The dry sound of scraping antlers on bark and wood. And in the far distance, from the other side of the lake, the whizzing of rifle shots.

Early one morning in his old winter sleeping place above the marsh, before either peeing or drinking water, he was licking his paws and listening. Dawn was breaking over the edge of the forest and the fog hovered over the treetops like grey smoke. Although he wasn't about to get up, there were sounds, still too far away to interpret, that disturbed him.

He didn't dare go off among the little pines and crouch down, though he needed to. If he licked his paws hard, the noise of the licking blocked out the distant sounds altogether. His ears had a respite, only to be assaulted anew, in loud bursts, as soon as he paused. Eventually he did get up and slink along the edge of the marsh towards the barn. There he lay back down and took in the scents. But the light breeze that was beginning to make the mist rise from the marsh was coming from off the lake. The sounds were from a different direction.

He didn't know what they were, but they seemed to be growing louder and more frequent. There was something up there along the ridges. It was in lots of places and he didn't know what it was, nor could he capture its scent.

Just then a fox skirted the marsh, running fast in a straight line. Twice the ribbon of his red fur was visible. Then he was gone. But the dog could tell he was fleeing. So he got up and moved behind the barn. A raven screeched high in the sky. It had seen something. Time after time it called out.

The dog heeded the warning and slipped down towards the cleared area. He began to cross it at a brisk pace; the wind was awakening, blowing off the lake. He didn't stop until he reached the beaver tarn. There was silence, but it wasn't a silence he trusted. He stood on the ridge above the tarn, waiting for the fickle morning breeze to turn so he could catch the scent of the danger coming from that direction, from the edge of the forest where the birds were making such a racket.

Then it came. A light, biting whiff to his sensitive nose. The smell of smoke. He turned tail and fled.

All morning he ran, looking for a way out. Now he knew the noise meant people. They had never before come from up above. They usually kept their loud bursts of noise close to the shore. They were being quiet, but little sounds that were not part of his knowledge of the forest told him where they were. Loud rustling. Sharp banging. He was prickly with fear when he worked out that there were many of them and they were far apart in places he could not identify. As he tried to get away, he kept encountering others who were fleeing as well. Hares rushed past. Game birds rose noisily, heading straight towards the lake, hurrying away from the transformed forest.

★

A dog. Excited barking.

He went rigid, lowering his belly to the ground. Never had he heard barking on this side. A thin yapping; it cohered into a ribbon of noise in the air, rising and falling. A dog tracking its prey. Loud and shrill. Then it sank again, coming closer.

He turned, bounding up the slope. Along with the

roaring in his ears he also heard a crackling sound. He never saw the man, but from the band of trees beyond a little grassy area, he caught a heavy scent. He changed direction again, rushing back the same way he had come, the barking of the dogs in his ears.

As he crossed the pasture he heard something large, running. Loud panting. He lowered himself into the blanket of leaves and grass so as not to be visible. The massive body rushed closer. Very close to him, it abruptly changed course.

It was the bull moose. Mouth wide open, tongue stiff. Inhaling and exhaling wheezily, gasping.

The moose was so close to him for an instant that the dog, lying flat in the grass, felt as if he were being singed by the smell and the bursts of air. As the moose rushed on towards the point he no longer heard panting, only the cracking of branches and brush. Just as the huge body plunged into the water, a dog appeared.

He dashed silently through the pressed-down tracks in the grass. When he reached the point he began to bark in a high-pitched tone. This was the sound of a dog in pursuit, almost a howl. The moment he reached the water the tone changed. It grew deeper. He was telling someone what was happening. He was wild with excitement. But he didn't follow the bull moose as it swam off across the lake.

The grey dog was about to sneak back up the slope towards the barn and beyond to make his escape, when a shot resounded. It came from so close by it hurt his ears.

For a few moments his senses exploded. He remembered nothing and was not aware of danger. When he could see and hear again he found himself lying pressed up against the trunk of a spruce.

He could feel the ground trembling from two directions. Someone was there, on the other side of the spruce. Out in the pasture a second moose was careering down the slope.

When the grey dog heard whoever was behind the spruce make a rattling sound, he bolted. In a panic, he dashed towards the point, following the moose, and crept under a windfallen tree. From his hiding place he could see the moose fall. He knew it must be the young female, though he wasn't entirely familiar with her scent. Blood foamed around her muzzle.

The black dog that had been pursuing the bull stopped barking and ran quickly towards her. When she heard him approaching she wobbled up and tried to reach the water.

Bright blood poured from her wounded lungs. When the dog reached her she plunged forward and toppled heavily into the lake.

The black dog barked, prancing along the shore. Otherwise there was silence. The moose lay in the water like a block of stone. Little waves sparkled and washed softly around her body.

It remained quiet. The black dog whined softly, pacing. In the trees, the birds that had gone silent now resumed their activities. Soft peeping and chirping could be heard, as if a new morning had dawned. The waves breaking on the shore and the leaves crackling in the wind overpowered these sounds. In the distance was the dull roar of the rapids, comforting and lulling.

The grey dog didn't move. He was downwind from the black one and took in his smell every time the other dog moved. He also knew the whereabouts of the man who had fired the shot. He was standing on the slope below the barn, though he hadn't made any noise for a long time now.

When the dog had lain still so long his body ached, he heard the man moving towards him. He was crossing the pasture, making no effort to hide. When he arrived at the cabin he stopped, putting down his rifle with a clatter. He continued with a lighter, more cautious step. The black dog barked.

Out at the point, the man began walking slowly; the dog could hear him breathing. He stopped right by the windfallen tree; the air was thick with his potent, compact smell. Then he waded out into the water. The grey dog rose up slightly on his stiff legs but did not dare flee. The black dog was still close by.

The man began to speak. There was static and beeping from his walkie-talkie. After a while he hung it on the branch of a birch tree, leaning his rifle against the trunk. There was rattling and rustling, followed by the smell of smoke.

The fire burned on the shore of the lake between two rocks. The man just sat idle, but he kept making sounds. After a while the water in the sooty aluminum coffee pot began to hum.

The dog lying under the windfallen tree listened without understanding. Many of the sounds were familiar from the fishing spots. They had reached him on the wind on bright nights and he had not forgotten them. They were frightening. He wanted to get away.

The unfamiliar male dog sat completely still beside the

man's backpack. His short coat gleamed. His eyelids were heavy in the warmth of the fire but his ears were pricked as if he were listening to something at a great distance.

The grey dog heard the sounds too. Other people were coming down. Soon voices could be heard from the pasture. He crept as far in towards the tumble of upturned roots as he could.

He couldn't attempt an escape without moving in the direction of the approaching men. There were too many of them and he didn't know exactly where each one was. Deep voices could be heard from all directions, the clang of metal and the flick of matches. Stiff fabric swished against straps.

They had other dogs with them. When they came closer they growled. The black one lying by the fire leapt up, his ragged ears rising. He rushed off towards the other dogs, then stopped in his tracks halfway and put his nose to the ground. He'd caught the scent of the grey dog.

Running excitedly, he took up the trail. When he came dangerously close the grey one rushed up and fled out towards the far end of the point. He heard the black dog in pursuit. Behind them the men were shouting and tying up the other loudly barking dogs.

He zigzagged through the undergrowth on the point. His heart was pounding; bursting with fear. There were no steep hills to hide in here, no endless marshes, no mountain forests. At the end of the point there were just cliffs on either side. More than once he ran down to the edge of the water and turned back. Finally he stopped. The black dog stopped too. They weren't far apart. The grey one lowered his head, ears pulled back, baring his teeth with a fierce expression. That was too much for the other dog. He attacked.

They fought, growling deeply all the time. The black dog's body was heavier and his legs shorter. He wasn't easily thrown off balance. He bit wherever he could reach, vicious warnings, while continuing to growl, urging his opponent to bare his neck and give up.

The grey one was still young, and emaciated. He'd never been in a fight before. But now he was fighting for his life. He bit back, wherever he could reach, and his bites were sharper than the black dog's. They didn't hear the voices shouting all around them. The men and the other dogs, on leashes, were there now, too. One man grabbed the hind legs of the black dog and pulled at him. He lost his balance and his jaws released their grip. Another man aimed a kick at the chest of the grey dog. They were separated. Someone managed to get the black foxhound on a leash, pressing a glove over the bleeding wound on his cheek.

The grey dog stood all alone on the lakeshore, facing the men and three dogs. His body was rigid. When one of the men began to approach he didn't flee, but pulled back his upper lip and lunged.

So many voices and bodies. He had to keep each individual in the crowd in sharp focus while he was looking for a hole to escape through. Then something happened that confused him.

All but one of the men withdrew. They left, taking the other dogs with them. He could still hear them among the trees. Only one man stayed behind, alone. But he didn't come closer. He went down on his knees. Then he lowered his head so neither his eyes nor his teeth were visible. A voice came out. It wasn't like the others. It murmured and clucked. It was a gentle stream of soft talking that awakened a strong urge in the young grey dog, in the midst of all his confusion.

Something might happen here. He didn't know what. He was still frightened. Every time the crouching man moved, the dog's muscles went taut. The voice, though, made him feel weak with longing. He wanted to run up to the man. But at the same time he was terrified.

So he sat down heavily on his bottom and started thumping his back paw against his neck, behind his ear. The motion made his chest ache. After some time he got up and moved to one side. His body was no longer so rigid. He could hear soft sounds and dogs whining from the woods. But instead of fleeing for his life he walked along the shore at a measured, leisurely pace. Once or twice he turned around to look at the crouching man, who was still talking, on and on, in a soft, lulling tone. When the grey dog was out of sight the man stood up and whistled for him. Short, high-pitched sounds.

The grey dog stopped. He was part of the way up the slope, heading for the pasture, and he knew he was visible. The whistling was like the lulling voice. He was drawn to it.

Deep inside, deep down, was everything that had happened between himself and the man. It had happened between a litter of puppies and a deep-voiced fellow who could shrink to half his own size by going down on his

knees. He had a voice that made them so excited they would pee all over the linoleum and nip at his sweater sleeves and fingertips.

It was not lost. It did not begin to happen again when the man whistled and called. But something shifted, moved.

He didn't go any farther than the barn. Once there he lay down and listened. He licked his coat thoroughly clean. He had a bleeding sore high up on one shoulder that his tongue couldn't reach. He tried rubbing it with one paw and then licking the paw clean. He was thirsty and would have wandered farther afield for water, would have gone all the way to the beaver tarn, enveloping himself in the silence, if it hadn't been for that whistling. The short, high-pitched sounds reached him off and on. His chest ached where he had been kicked. He wanted to lie still for a long time. It hurt when he breathed.

He didn't see the men pull the female moose up out of the lake. But the sickening smells of blood and excrement came to him on the wind. When the men left, carrying heavy loads and taking the dogs, straining at their leashes, he withdrew. But he came back to listen. All he could hear was the rustling of the leaves and the little waves breaking against the stones on the shore.

When he walked down to the lake the injured rib in his chest ached; it hurt more when he moved. But thirst drove him. Lapping up water, he stood with his paws in the lake, feeling the chill spread through him, deadening the pain. He walked a little farther out, letting himself be numbed.

Then he heard the whistling again. He turned fast, trying to run up out of the water, but he stumbled, hunched and stiff. Once he was out of the lake he didn't stop until he was halfway up to the barn. The man was still at the spot where they had cut up the moose. He'd been completely still until that moment.

The soft whistling kept the dog there. He lay in the grass listening to what the man was doing. Most of his tasks were silent ones, but now and then he would break dry branches or split a log. The smell of smoke wafted up. And that occasional whistling.

Once they both appeared in the open. The dog stood up in the grass. The man stepped forward to the edge of the birch brushwood that extended from the point up towards the pasture. After a while they both withdrew again, one silently, the other whistling softly.

Late that afternoon two boats came and collected the man and the moose meat, which he had butchered into manageable pieces. The man paced uneasily. When he left with the other men he was whistling, but the dog didn't let himself be seen. When the voices and the sound of the oars in the water were gone he went down. He was extremely tense and agitated by the whiffs of scent crossing every which way in the rough terrain. Now, though, he was alone at the point.

At the spot where the moose had been slaughtered there were patches of blood but no remains. He sniffed around. The smells awakened the hunger pangs in his belly. But he was tired and his injured chest hurt. He couldn't hunt in the pasture when his body wouldn't respond. He licked at the patches of blood but found nothing to eat. In the end he wandered back up to the cabin and rested at the foot of the steps. He lay very still, curled tightly into his own dizziness and pain.

At dusk he went back down. He walked on stiff legs and with slow, jerky movements. There was a strong wind blowing from off the mountains to the west. It had picked up as night fell, and it washed through his coat and cleared his nose and ears after all the confusion of the day and the jumble of scents and loud noises.

Then he caught a whiff of the man. He knew he wasn't there. But his smell was. It was at the spot where he'd been fighting with that black dog; a compact odour, not just a residual scent from the morning. His instinct was to turn tail, but his muscles wouldn't obey. Then he smelled the blood. He moved closer to something dark between the stones. Next to it he found the food.

He ate, pressed low and tail uncurled. It didn't take long to devour the pile of meat. Before he hobbled off, he sniffed every bit of the fabric, its familiar smell.

That night he slept up in the cleared area, where he could hear all the sounds coming off the lake, even the most distant ones. His belly was heavy from the meat. He slept for long stretches and the pain receded. At dawn he went back down to the spot where the man had left his jacket spread across the stones alongside the pile of chopped moose lung. Sniffing the whole area thoroughly, he found a few scraps he'd missed.

It was a windy day. He couldn't hear any noise from the forest, no gunshots. He lay still for so long that when he got up there were yellow birch leaves stuck to his coat.

The man returned that evening, rowing across. The creak of the oarlocks cut through the wind. As he stepped out of the boat he whistled and talked, but he didn't stay long. When darkness was falling he pushed the boat out into the lake and it vanished, along with the creaking and splashing. The grey dog lay in the clearing, ears pricked, following the journey.

There was food down there. The man had put it where the wind would carry the scent to the cleared area. The dog had revealed himself there for an instant, a grey-black mask and a pair of attentive ears in the undergrowth.

★

Things had gone quiet all around the pasture. Only the softest voices were still there. He heard the chirping of the titmice and the soft calls of the bullfinches from among the trees. The Siberian jays fluttered gently among the birch leaves, which fell even on windless days. The aspen leaves were ready to fall. Sometimes on frosty mornings he heard soft clicking sounds as they snapped loose.

The water that had filled green leaves and made the grass grow tall was receding. The blanket of pasture was withering and turning yellow. At the roots, where the soil was still damp and warm, the mouldering process began, working on leaves and whatever else was on the ground. Everything that happened now took place deep down, and from the earth rose the heavy, powerful scent of decomposition. When the rain began to sweep in off the ocean beyond the mountains, the pasture became a brown place of rough grass and rotting stalks. It was silent there. The short-eared owl rarely swooped, and eventually it flew away. Not even the vixen caught any voles.

The dog's shoulder healed but his bruised rib continued to ache in the cold weather. Most of the time he lay still, though he had to guard the food spot out at the point and keep the vixen away. She sniffed around, sticking her pointy snout in between the stones where there were still patches of blood. He moved awkwardly from the pain in his ribcage, so he was careful not to rush at her, just letting himself be seen so she wouldn't become overconfident. The fur on his

shoulder was long again. He raised his head and chest, and she ran off. But she would soon be back unless he stayed out at the point, guarding the spot.

The man arrived late each afternoon. After a few days he moved the food spot over to the cabin, laying the chopped entrails in a bowl at the bottom of the outside steps, his rain-soaked jacket across them. Before he headed home he sat in the boat for a long time, whistling and talking.

★

Rain and days passed by. One blue-sky day when the sun was warm but the frost was thick and the air still, the boat appeared in the morning instead. The man pulled it further up than usual. Glancing towards the cleared area, he noted a pair of alert ears following the noise made by the bottom of the boat scraping on the damp gravel. He walked past the cookhouse and up to the cabin with loud steps, tossing his backpack down with a thump that reverberated in the still air. He settled in, with slamming doors and groaning window frames. He lit the stove, knowing that the gusts of smoke, and later the smell of coffee, would reach all the way up to the cleared area. But the dog didn't appear. In the evening the man put out food as usual, but this time right on the steps. Then he shut himself inside the cabin. In the morning the food remained untouched.

All day he busied himself around the pasture. He felled birch saplings and repaired a broken pane in the cookhouse window. Although he could see no signs of life up at the clearing, he aimed his whistling and talk in that direction. Late that evening he left the cabin, putting food on the steps. He had also left a door open, the one leading into the hall where the woodpile was. He put a blanket on the floor next to the soggy jacket, and then rowed away with long, creaking strokes. Yellow birch leaves floated in the water along the shore. Now and then he rested on the oars, listening and looking up towards the top of the rise behind the grey cabin, where the stove was going cold now that he'd left.

Dusk was falling. The man felt the pull of the black water as he rowed along the point. The last stretch across the lake he just glided in the silent darkness. Not until he heard stones scraping against the bottom of the boat was he brought back from the fantasy that he was dipping the oars into an indestructible thick, black mass. When he'd left the

boat and put on his backpack, he stood for a long time staring across at the point. He thought he sensed a presence
moving along the edge of the woods. When he had stood
there for ages, staring into the shifting, flickering darkness,
he thought he saw a black mask, imagined that for an instant
the two of them were staring at each other.

*

The vixen had gone in and peed on the jacket. It was bright
daylight when the dog cautiously approached the cabin steps.
The open door and the dim interior made him tense and on
his guard. A powerful smell of the fox and her piss came
from the doorway.

Stiff and awkward from fear and the pain in his ribcage, he
climbed the stairs. No food. And that taunting smell of fox.
Bowl licked clean and everywhere, in every nook and
cranny, she'd poked her pointed snout. She'd even pissed on
the jacket, like a male.

His blood was hot and pounding, his skin prickled under
his coat. He, too, peed on the wet fabric, then climbed back
down the steps, walking a wide arc in front of the cabin,

marking his territory with distinct splashes. He had neither eaten nor had anything to drink for a long time. His urine was yellow and pungent. He was very thirsty, needed to go down to the lake, but his watchfulness and a readily aroused, stinging sense of anger kept him there. After a while he lay down at the foot of the steps, soaking up some morning sun. His eyes never left the little birches on the far side of the pasture where she tended to emerge when she left the den.

When the sunlight had moved beyond the top step in front of the cabin, he was still lying there. Towards midday he went down to the lake and drank his fill, then went back up again, lying on the steps instead, to have a better view. When he lay still and breathed calmly he was in less pain. He lay out of the wind coming off the lake; his coat was dry. The insects that flickered past were late ones that had not yet found their death or a crack in which to spend the winter. Fragile wings flashed by.

He had to rely on his vision that day. The wind was against him, blowing in the direction of the vixen's den. She had a litter of growing cubs. They could turn up anywhere he looked. He kept an eye out for movements, for shapes that changed.

He was on guard but calm. Deep inside his watchfulness there was anger without the least bit of fear. It lay there, poised. It could raise the fur on the ridge of his neck and make his front half large and threatening without his even getting up. A dull, rolling growl also lay there, ready. He used it once or twice when he saw shadows moving in the blurry area between grass and yellowing ash shoots.

Late in the afternoon he heard the boat. So he clambered down the steps in spite of the pain, and stood over by the cookhouse to watch the man disembark. He stood in the open. When the man caught sight of him he stopped, stood perfectly still and whistled, softly and gently. After a while he walked up the grassy slope. The dog moved out of sight.

He hung around the slope in the cleared area all the time the man was there. When he was alone again he went back to the cabin, gobbled up the contents of the bowl and lay back down to watch and wait. Occasionally he had to go off and relieve himself; the food had made his stomach uneasy. The first few days most of it had gone right through him, but he was better now. He never went farther than to the raspberry patch alongside the cabin. After doing his business he would lie back down on the steps.

The grass was always wet at this time of year, and it was hard for him to extricate his paws. There wasn't enough sun to dry up the pasture. Aspen leaves flashed in the rays of sun, floating down like stiff wings, flight without life. In the grass they became mottled, and the brown spots soon grew larger.

Brown had taken over. Under the blanket of grass, everything was decaying; the spreading patches emitted a heavy scent. The late summer darkness hung in the tops of the rowans; frost had stripped away the dense leaves and berries. Now the leaves were falling from the treetops into the grass, decomposing silently. Berries hung bright from leafless branches.

Along the shore of the inlet, sallow stalks stood straight and tall. Now that the leaves had fallen he could see the water and catch a glimpse of the birds down there. When the strokes from the man's oars scared up a wood grouse on the point, the grey dog followed its flight from his lookout on the steps. No leaves blocked his view. The cock rose, neck long, wingstrokes quick and invisible, a heavy weight flying in a straight line into the dark spruce forest.

Wind squalls blew beneath a dense cloud cover. The

mountains were never visible any longer. Wisps of cloud scuttled above the lake and the tarn.

Twilight was brief. Night fell like a black curtain, too fine for the eye to perceive, merging with the darkness of the rocks and the darkness dwelling in the spruces. The gusts of wind ripped at the tops of the grass, rough and dull, like blunted knives. The heads of the starwort were dry now, stalks tufted, thin and brittle as skeletons. The cow parsley plants still had black seeds on their brittle ribs, but the shrew mice could no longer climb them in the wind.

★

For the dog, the days disappeared slowly, like leaves sinking in water. He forgot them all and stored them deep inside. He no longer hunted. He waited and watched.

The man brought his food. He didn't come every single day and no longer from the open part of the lake where the wind tossed the water up against the stones. He would land the boat in the marshy inlet. The wind carried off the sounds and scents; often the man would appear unexpectedly from the undergrowth at the edge of the pasture. The dog would

rise from his spot and move away stiffly. As soon as the man
had left, he would go back down and eat and continue his
watch. He never saw so much as a shadow of the vixen. But
he never forgot her.

Between himself and the man something happened every
time they met: the voice and the food. That was the good
part. It was a warm stomach and a pleasant sensation sifting
like strong sunlight through his fur. It touched nerves and
awakened memories with no images.

The scent of fox remained in the mouldy jacket. When he
came inside, his nose clear from the strong wind, he smelled
it. That was the bad part. It made him edgy. Between him
and the man there was this as well: he had to keep the fox
away. Not until the man's boots could be heard tramping
through the overgrown pasture could he abandon his post.
He stretched his back legs, squatting down to do what he'd
needed to do for hours. But he seldom went farther than to
the barn nowadays, although his pain had let up and no
longer slowed him down.

The wind rose to storm strength. One night the rumbling
in the tops of the spruces intensified until the dark night
roared from a hole no one could see. The lake thrashed and

thrashed against the stones, lifting heavy logs of loose timber far up onto the shore.

He lay in the dark cabin by the woodpile, his body tightly curled around muzzle and paws, listening through the open door to the cracking of branches and the crashing of tree trunks. Although the wind was coming from the other side, the door kept slamming on the wire loop the man had made. It jerked all night long, creaking, trying to come loose along with the other things being blindly tossed about outside.

Day arrived with bright light and a cold wind under a sky with scuttling wisps of cloud. There was a glimmer of blue beneath them, and now and then the sun glistened in high breakers on the lake. He went out to pee, and then headed down to the lake to drink at the shore that was sheltered from the wind. The grass lay in brown drifts. It caught at his paws as if wanting to drag him down into the wetness. Gusts of wind tore at his coat, combing it up sharply on end.

The storm that tore at his fur was not merely cold and unpleasant. It robbed him of his dignity and composure. He needed to present a strong, cohesive front to the world. But now, shaggy and hunched down, he was being buffeted towards the water, half fearful, half angry, and vulnerable. By the time he headed back up, though, he was whole again, although his ears were still pressed back and the white fur on his chest was matted.

For two more days the wind continued to blow. He curled up around his hunger, not leaving the cabin to hunt. One cold morning when the tail end of the storm was still surging against the rocks on the shore, the man returned. The dog didn't see him until he was at the bottom of the slope between cabin and lake. They hadn't been this close to each other since the dogfight at the shore. But this time the man didn't crouch down and he didn't say anything.

If the dog left the steps he would have to approach the figure standing down there. Or he could rush into the tall, straight raspberry canes alongside the cabin. From there he could sidle off towards the cleared area.

He rose slowly, standing still, his back legs bent. His ears were perked. The fur on his back had risen and darkened to a sharp strip running like a fin all the way to the root of his tail. The mane of fur around his neck and muzzle was also on end. His slanted eyes in the stiff, black mask stared at the man. But he still hadn't moved.

There was a flutter. The last brittle leaves from the crown

of an aspen had resisted the storm but now let go in a puff of wind that blew through the branches. Perhaps the man thought it was a bird taking flight. He took his eyes off the dog.

And the dog went down the steps. He descended in three quick leaps, with no limp and no trace of his ribcage injury. He stopped at the bottom, suddenly unfurling his tightly coiled tail. It twitched.

The man made a sound: exhaling. The grey dog flicked his tail again. His head was cocked and he'd relaxed his ears. His smooth brow creased straight across. Twisting, he moved in an arc down towards the man, simultaneously approaching and keeping his distance. In spite of being out of practice, he looked genuinely friendly. The hair on his back had settled down, without depriving him of his dignity or composure. His curly tail, almost floppy, was wagging. The whole hind part of him was in motion and he took little tripping steps in smaller and smaller loops around the man.

That was when the man started to talk. He muttered and mumbled, head turned aside, moving in the direction of the cabin. When he went into the hall, putting pieces of bread and meat in the enamel bowl, the dog sat nearby, staring intently in through the doorway. He listened to the crinkling of the plastic bag and to the soft, rhythmic voice. When the man had gone back down to the shore, the dog went straight up and ate. For the first time he ate while being watched. He gobbled the food; the enamel bowl rattled against the floorboards. When it was empty he didn't take the time to lick it clean. He ambled out, settling in partway up the pasture slope, watching the man.

★

A series of bright, clear days followed. The wind was sharp and churned up the lake, but only on the surface, and never enough to prevent him from hearing the creaking of the oarlocks as the man came rowing.

One evening he barked when he heard the boat. He wasn't accustomed to barking. His voice cracked and his yapping became a howl. Soon, though, it carried well.

He would bark out across the lake now. Sometimes when he heard the creaking of the oars, sometimes just because he had the urge. He would sit out at the end of the point listening to his yaps reverberate against the cliffs by the narrows.

Now he would be standing in the trees by the lakeshore when the man landed his boat. His curly tail wagged; he paced eagerly, twisting and turning and letting his ears relax. His throat produced sounds he hadn't really mastered. Out of him came yaps and yelps. When he heard the rattling of the enamel bowl against the bottom of the boat he would tramp back and forth under the alder bushes. Soon he came closer.

The man had started feeding him where he landed the boat. He would put the bowl down on the stones by the shore, then head up towards the cabin by himself. He'd stop about halfway up the slope, watching the dog eat. The bowl jumped on the stones. Sometimes it was in the water by the time he had finished. The man would wade out to get it later, talking softly all the while. The dog would be sitting on the slope by then, watching. They switched places comfortably and sometimes they were very close when their paths crossed.

One evening he left the bowl in the boat. He'd landed it stern first, close to a flat stone. The dog hesitated briefly, then stood on the stone and ate. The next evening the bowl was in the bottom of the boat.

When he had eaten they would take a walk. The man's boots trampled down the tufted brown grass. The dog ran in big circles in front of and behind him. He stopped and waited at the edge of the marsh. His mask looked very black there, against the fluttering leaves in the sparse birches.

When darkness crept up on the spruce forest the man would leave. The dog followed the boat from the shore, walking all the way out to the end of the point. He stood there listening to the scraping and banging of the boat landing on the other side. Chains jangled. There was rattling when the man pulled in the oars and a sliding sound as he dragged the boat ashore. All these sounds were now familiar. He knew what came next: the pounding of footsteps on the hard, dry, grassy soil. Then there was silence. He stayed sitting there for a while. The water at the narrows purled, and in the distance was the roar of the rapids, blocking other sounds from the mysterious opposite shore where the footsteps had vanished. He went back to the pasture and climbed the steps to the cabin, going in through the open door, held with a hook. He would lie in the opening and wait. That was his place.

He was the one who waited.

★

One day the man arrived in the morning. The wake rippled the water, creating a pattern of light and shadow. The dog sat at the edge of the woods, listening. He was uncertain and had to scratch his ear. He thumped for quite a while, sensing it was the wrong time of day. His stomach told him it was wrong, and the light falling from the wrong direction. He couldn't hear the rattling enamel bowl, either. The man walked right up to the cabin. He looked around, squinting; the light was so sharp the rowan berries on the leafless branches gleamed bright against the sky.

The grey dog stopped scratching and followed, bounding cheerfully, keenly excited, like one who has been waiting for a long time and now senses the wait is nearly over.

The man strode on; he was happy, too. He radiated good cheer; it was in the calm morning air, without him saying anything.

Above the pasture, where the wetlands began, the meadowsweet was more than waist high. The soggy ground had a strong smell. The dog followed, engulfed in meadowsweet. When they reached the marsh the man stopped, looking for hoof tracks. He'd put a salt lick at this spot during the summer. It was gone now, but the ground under the pole was still salty. The dog had been there too, sniffing and digging. Now he waited at a distance. The minute the man moved on he bounded after him.

He criss-crossed the marsh, following scents and gusts of airborne smells playfully, without any real intent to hunt. He kept his eyes on the man, as he strode calmly across the higher ground. When he entered the woods the dog ran up behind him and followed at his heels on the path, ears alert and tail tightly coiled.

They crossed a second marsh, after which they headed sharply uphill towards a little slope of crooked, lichen-clad birches. At the top, the man stood still for a long time, staring out across the marshes and the parcels of forest land, across the lake water gleaming so bright it was difficult to fix one's gaze on the huge sheet of pure light. He looked towards the blue mountains over in Norway, their slopes dotted with snow. The dog sat a little way behind him. His nose was sensitive to what the gusts of wind carried with them, but he certainly wasn't looking at the view. He sat there squinting.

The moss was bright, and the sun caught in the yellowing field of grasses. Around tree stumps there were ripening clusters of lingonberries, and every single shiny leaf among them stood out as if it had just been created. The man pulled off handfuls of lingonberries, letting them run through his fingers down into the moss. His gaze wandered. Sometimes it played on nearby things, on the ground and the grass. Sometimes it sought things far away, off in the marshes, and where the forest became sparser. For a few minutes he looked at the distant ridges and mountain peaks, jagged and blue, and at the bright light on the lake. Then his gaze returned to what was nearby, resting on the stumps and the berries.

The dog sat, ears cocked. He followed what was happening in the distance, mostly the doings of the birds in the trees; once a snapping branch, a crashing hoof made his ears perk even more and his shiny, black nose wriggle.

They both heard a game bird rise, possibly a large wood grouse. The man looked at the dog, saying a couple of words. The dog's tail began to twitch and he sat even more attentively.

The sun warmed him. It shone down on his curly white chest; it felt good. This morning there was no pain. He grew sleepy in the sun and lay down, forepaws extended. He kept his head up and his ears perked, his nose sniffing, but his eyes were shut for longer and longer spells.

The man lay down, too. He'd turned around, saying something in a soft voice, waking the dog from his sun-slumber. Then he stretched out in the moss on his stomach. His face vanished. His voice was gone, his gaze, the teeth that gleamed.

The dog jumped up. Initially tense, he moved slowly toward the man, tail straightening. Then he pulled it back in with a twitch. He ran up, poking the man's neck and ears with his muzzle. When the man rolled over, the dog licked his face. Eagerly, his tongue swept all over it. When the man rose onto his elbows, the grey dog lay down, belly-up. His insect-bitten stomach glistened in the sun.

Now the man spoke to him again in the same way he had done when they had met during the moose hunt. He put one hand on the dog's neck behind his ear and scratched his short fur hard.

After a while the two of them rose, the dog leaping up with a bound. When he had shaken himself he was composed again. They began to hike back down. He was happy. That was clear from the way he ran in circles in the marsh. He ran much more than he had to, out of sheer joy. When the man began to laugh at him he ran even faster. He took off at great speed, kicking up a nasty smell in the mire.

When does something end?

Perhaps never. There's always something else after it. Hunting days follow with sun and strong wind, and lazy days of rest, head against forepaws, listening to the heavy rain streaming through the branches of the aspen and drumming on the tin roof. Long, sleepy days when wooden walls make clicking noises in the cold, and spring days of dripping water and chirping birds, when the very air seems to come to life, tickling nose and ears.

This tale will not end as long as a dog's strong heart goes on beating, as it is likely to do for quite a few years to come.

They called him Plucky. That name came to the man as he rowed back that Sunday morning when he had been allowed to touch him for the first time.

People asked how he managed to get him tied up. But he

129

never used a rope or a leash. The dog had come of his own accord.

★

The man often told the story of how he'd started putting out food at the lakeshore and then in the boat. One day when the dog had become accustomed to standing in the boat he had carefully shoved it out. The dog had crouched down, ears pulled back. But they got across without him trying to jump out.

He also spoke often of how they made their way home through the village. The dog had walked right at the edge of the woods, often entirely out of sight. Now and then he peeked out. Almost invisible, he followed his master.

Like some damn cat, the man said.

★

The dog came to love sitting by the stove. His old injuries sometimes ached, and the older he got the more he loved the sunshine, the warmth from the sun on the rag rug on the front steps, and the heat of the white enamel Husqvarna stove in which they burned birch wood. He liked her, too, the one who put down his bowls of food. When no one was looking he would jump up on the wooden kitchen settee and lie on her sweater.

He was quick to learn what he wasn't allowed to do. The mother dog knew. But she no longer punished him. There was no need. He copied her.

★

One winter day a flock of migrating moose crossed the clearing on the other side of the ridge. The mother dog was loose and the grey dog followed her. They cornered three moose on the marsh. The snow reached way up over their bellies, so they couldn't move fast enough to prevent the moose from getting away. The flock dispersed and the dogs were left with just one, a yearling with long, white legs.

After two hours the mother dog had had enough. But the grey dog kept it up. When his master came skiing to call him off, he had been barking for five hours. That was when the man realised he was a very special dog. That's what he said later, over and over again.

He started training him, first on the ski track and then behind his bicycle. In September he took him along hunting for the first time. He wouldn't chase his prey very far, but the man said that was an advantage. Saved you standing around waiting for a dog that had gone his own way.

That first season they shot five moose he had hunted down, four bulls and a calf. There would be more. He'd earned his name, the man said.

Now he was able to take him in the car when he was going to meet the others, and he could also put a collar and leash on him. Not even the radio scared him any more.

But he remained a one-man dog and no one could touch him but his master, and the woman who put down his food bowl by the kitchen sink. Both of them also knew they should speak gently. A raised, angry voice would make him retreat and not reappear for a long time.

He was constantly watchful. Often he sat upright on the front porch or out at the top of the steep hill on which the farmhouse perched, ears and nose attentive. He followed things that happened far away. The brown, squinting eyes in the black mask monitored movements in the leaves and the grass.

★

Even indoors he was on his guard. Often they thought he looked as if he were listening for something, though they couldn't imagine what.

They would put a hand on his head and talk to him, but he would pull away and settle back down somewhere he would not be disturbed.

He remained alone in his waiting.

★

The tale ends there. No one knows what he was listening for or what he had been through out there where no one had been able to see him.

No one even knows whether there's a word for whatever it is he's waiting for.